FOR SUCH A TIME...

BY JOYCE LESLEY KEATING

ACKNOWLEDGEMENTS

Many thanks to "Creative Commons for artwork used on the cover. I am also indebted to the NHS website for the information about cancer treatments in current use.

DEDICATION

I was lucky to come in contact with people who made the stories of the Bible heroes come alive. Two in particular stand out, Miss Janet Hill, my youth group leader, and Revd Jimmie Song, the vicar in Matlock Bath. I was also introduced to the great writings of C S Lewis by Ruth Ring, a teacher at my school.

Zak, the storyteller in this book, combines them all.

FORWARD

Well, here we are in the middle of a pandemic so where are all the superheroes when you need them? One of the things we notice if we look back is that most of the really effective heroes are just ordinary folk who step up to the plate and never give up until the job is done. My own particular "Look up to guy" was Douglas Bader, a flying ace of World War Two. Not so much for his amazing skills, but because he volunteered to go back in the RAF when he had already lost his legs. Amazingly, when finally captured by the enemy he tried to escape. In fact he did it so many times they took away his "tin legs" and he still tried to get away without them. That kind of spirit will bring us through anything.

Hitler was thwarted in his attempt to wipe out the Jews but funnily enough many others before him had also tried the same thing. Usually the attacks came when they had strayed away from their faith. Only when they finally sought help from God was a hero raised up from among them. These are some of the stories of the amazing feats of those ordinary people. Each chapter is a separate short story of one of those characters embedded in the account of a teacher's life which is entirely fictitious. Perhaps I can add the opening lines used by the medieval storyteller in my book "Christmas of the Storyman",

Here are the tales I present for your delight. May the Lord be pleased with everything I make up and add His Blessing to all that is true.

CHAPTER ONE: BIG SISTERS CAN BE USEFUL

Zak followed the ringleaders down the crowded street and into the dingy coffee bar they always dropped into after school. He bought one of the sludgy coffees and a dubious looking bun before he went over to their table. Hooking an extra stool over with one leg, he plonked the drink and plate onto the table and sat down. Their gobsmacked expressions turned to guilt and unease as he simply stared at them. Finally he said quietly,

"Well, what was all that about? In my history classes you are the best group I have. What turned you into monsters overnight? I helped out with that RE class because Angie is ill and it turned into a shambles, the worst hour of my life. I want an explanation."

While they stared at each other he bit into the bun and hastily washed down the awful taste with the grotty coffee. Finally, nudged by everyone else, Julie spoke up,

"We hate it. It's boring. We don't believe any of that rubbish."

Zak broke in,

"Excuse me! You didn't give me a chance to teach anything so how could it be boring?"

"Well Ange the Angel's lessons were."

He let the nickname pass, having heard it before, and thought for a moment,

"What counts as exciting?"

For a few minutes they tumbled over each other to talk about their gaming, Marvel's avengers and the superheroes they all loved. Zak's eyes gleamed. He had them.

"Suppose I end each lesson with a superhero story. Will you work for me as well in RE as you do in history?"

Enthusiastic nods and high fives sealed the deal. Sure enough, the following Monday they sat through his overview of world faiths and noted down websites to read up the homework. Then they settled back eagerly to hear the first story.

oOo

"Imma, why do the Egyptians hate us so much?"

"I don't think they do, Miri love. Pass me that bowl of water and the cleaning cloth."

Still puzzled, I went back to grinding the barley grains for the day's bread. Then I stopped again to ask Imma,

"If that's so why do they make us work so hard for them to build their store cities, Rameses, and Pithom and now On. Abba says they have to make their own bricks as well and still keep up with the day's quota."

Jochebed snorted in amusement.

"They're afraid of us, that's why. When Joseph brought our ancestors here to escape the great famine, there were about seventy of us. Now how many do you think there are?"

I thought of all our settlements scattered through the Goshen district and said,

"Thousands, probably."

"Well, there you are then. Wouldn't you be afraid if you were them? And please hurry up with that bread or we will have no meal tonight."

Hurriedly I tipped the flour into our biggest bowl. I fetched the seor, the starter made of old dough left out to absorb the yeasts from the air and added two measures of it to the flour, and some goat's milk. As I kneaded the mixture and left it to rise I wondered what it would be like to live in a land of our own. Shrugging off such fanciful ideas I guessed it would take some sort of miracle for that to happen and went back to cleaning the smudges of flour off the old wooden table.

Later in the day I took the bread from the oven and set it to cool under an old clean cloth and went back to stirring the stew. It was only lentils but the onions, leeks and garlic in it made it smell really good. Staring across the field I noticed Shiphrah, my mother's friend, trudging up the path.

"Imma, your friend is coming."

"Is there enough of that stew for all of us, Miri?

"Yes, I'll serve it while you two chat."

Soon, we were all eating and discussing the news Shiphrah had brought. I poured us some of the crushed fruit juice and listened, horrified, while our midwife friend told us the latest orders she had been given. Apparently the Egyptians were now so frightened of us that they had stepped up their campaign to reduce our numbers. At first, the midwives had been asked to kill the male children as they were born. All of them thought this was a hideous crime so they simply ignored the orders. They all claimed the babies were already born before they got there. Now, families were being told to throw all the boys that were born into the river.

Imma went deathly pale and clutched her middle. Aha, Aaron, my older brother, and I already suspected she was having another baby but she hadn't talked about it to us yet.

"NO!" She got her determined face on. "It's wicked. We have to think of some way round it. Thank you for telling us. Now, you had better go back before you are missed."

By the time I had finished washing the bowls we had used Imma seemed to have recovered and when Abba and Aaron pushed open the door she smiled a welcome. Glowing embers in the stove had kept the stew hot for them and soon they were scooping it up with some of the newly baked bread.

"Miri, will you and Aaron go and fetch water, there is washing I need to do later?"

I opened my mouth ready to argue that there was already plenty, but her glare and a barely perceptible nod at Abba's back told me she wanted time alone with him. My brother started to say he was tired but I grabbed his arm and dragged him outside. Once he started arguing about something there was no shutting him up so it was best not to let him start.

We sat for a moment on a pile of old planks while I told him about the Pharaoh's new rules. Suggesting that he slept outside for a while to give Abba and Imma chance to talk, I took the leather bucket and trudged to the dyke. There was plenty of water as this season the river was quite high so water was still coming through the channels for the crops. It didn't take me long to fill up the old stone trough we used for storage. Thinking that they needed more time, I continued fetching water for the animals and then set about watering the plot where our vegetables grew. It was getting dark and I was worn out. Aaron had already gone back inside so I edged my way through the door, unrolled my sleeping mat and was soon fast asleep.

No one mentioned the conversation in the days that followed and life continued its usual pattern of work and sleep. Soon, there was no hiding the fact that Imma was having a baby. Perhaps it was the added worry of what would happen if it were a boy, but she was very poorly most days. Shiphrah came when she could and left herbs to put in hot water, advising her to rest as much as possible. Well, I was old enough to look after things and so I did, taking over her jobs as well as my own.

It was a very difficult and scary few months. Another girl would not be a problem but what if it were to be a boy? Abba and Imma were determined to save its life and they included me in the scheme they thought up.

When the baby was born it was easy to pretend it was a girl and keep it wrapped up. We introduced "her" to our relatives and friends. As "she" grew bigger it was only a matter of time until our secret got out and Imma was ordered to throw our beautiful baby into the river.

Big Dave butted in,

"Sir, I can't believe you're telling us the story of Moses; Ange the Angel told us it hundreds of times."

Zak opened his mouth to reply, but Julie beat him to it. With a great thump to his shoulder she said,

"Shurrup you dozy goat, can't you tell he isn't the hero of this, his sister is. I want to hear the rest of it. Turning to face Zak, who daren't let his amusement show, she said,

"Carry on , sir."

He cleared his throat, attempting not to laugh and continued.

That's when the clever plan came into operation. Imma had prepared a little woven basket covered in pitch all over the outside so it was waterproof. The poor baby was placed in it and lowered into the river. My part was to follow along and see what happened to it. What with jumping drainage ditches and working round thick clumps of reeds I was trailing a long way behind. As I worked my way round trees and bushes I heard excited giggles and shouts. I parted the bushes to watch and listen, realising it was a swimming party from the palace. They spotted the basket and one of the maids grabbed it as it floated past.

They realised straight away that it was one of the Hebrew children who was supposed to be killed. I held my breath. Just then my lovely little brother gave a loud, tearful yell. They made soothing noises and he smiled a toothless grin. The princess was enchanted and began making plans to keep the baby. As they discussed how it could be looked after, I thought quickly and strolled up to join in the conversation,

"I know of a woman who could nurse him for you. Shall I fetch her?"

Given the go ahead I raced back to Imma and told her. We hugged each other and I led her back to the group waiting on the bank. Jochebed bowed very low, saying,

"You sent for me, your Highness?"

In great excitement the young Royal explained how they had found the child and how adorable it was.

"I shall raise him as my own, but until he is old enough to live in the palace with me, would you be willing to nurse him for me?

Jochebed pretended to hesitate and then agreed. What happened next astonished me as the Princess offered to pay Imma well for her trouble! Barely containing her grin, Imma murmured,

"As you will, your Highness," and picked up the basket. We both backed away then turned and walked sedately until we were out of sight beyond the bend in the river. Carefully, we put the basket down then hugged each other, dancing around till we were breathless.

"It worked!" I crowed. "Not only is he safe but you are getting paid to look after him. Nobody will dare to touch him because he belongs to the Princess."

"Miri, your quick thinking saved him. God must have helped you. I am sure the baby will grow up to do great things one day."

Probably because we knew our time with him was limited, we crammed as much into every day as we could. He grew into a tall and sturdy little boy. Aaron showed him how to keep watch over the sheep, finding grazing for them. I let him help me bake and fetch water for the livestock. Each night, we told him stories about our people. There was adventurous Father Abraham, tricksy Jacob and Joseph who brought everyone to Egypt and saved everyone in the great famine. He listened so intently, remembering everything and asking questions. He watched Imma and I making food and saving old clothes for those who were ill and could not work. He took everything in.

Then the day came. At the age of twelve he was counted old enough to work so now the Princess sent for him. Imma thought she would never see him again but I said,

"He will find a way to come back to us. Just wait and see."

At first, he was kept in to learn about the Egyptian ways and receive lessons as the other boys in the palace did, but gradually they trusted him more and he made regular visits to us. At first we were afraid he would begin to look down on us when he had learned the fancy palace ways, but no, instead he grew angry at the poverty he saw around him. His life of luxury was a great contrast but he seemed uneasy with it and clung to us when it was time to go back.

One fateful day he rushed in and begged some of Aaron's old, ragged clothes. When I looked bewildered he explained; the words tumbling over each other, he was in such a rush. After his last visit he had spotted one of the Egyptian overseers beating one of the poor workers. He had intervened a bit too enthusiastically and had killed the overseer. Hastily checking there was nobody nearby he had buried the man and gone on his way. Then, today on his way to see us, he had come across two of our own people fighting. When he tried to persuade them to calm down one of them had sneeringly asked if he was going to kill them like he had the Egyptian.

"So, Miri, the story must have got out. Pharaoh will kill me. I will have to leave."

"But where will you go?"

"Best I don't tell you as they are bound to look here for me. Say goodbye to Imma and Abba and Aaron. I will try to come back one day." He grabbed the bag with some bread and cheese I got for him and raced away.

Yes, there was a fuss, but after a while it all died down and we began to hope Moses would come back. But the months turned into years and I thought of him from time to time, somehow sure that we would meet again. In fact, almost thirty years had passed when Aaron came to me white faced and with staring eyes. God had spoken to

19

him! Apparently the time had come for Moses to return as God was going to rescue our people and he was going to use Moses to do it. Aaron gulped,

"I am to sneak out into the desert and meet Moses then come back with him and help him. Apparently I talk so much that I can do the talking for both of us!"

I couldn't help it, I roared with laughter at the look on his face and remembering the times he had sweet-talked himself out of awkward situations. If anyone was just made for a job, he was.

Zak paused for a gulp of water. You all know how the story works out. The brothers did confront Pharaoh and after ten plagues sent by God the king agreed to let the whole nation go. There is about five minutes left so check over what you have to do for homework.

"Sir," said Julie, "didn't Miri come into the story anymore?"

"Why yes, but it's not all good. I've just time for this last bit."

Crossing the Red Sea on dry ground with all the waters piled up by a fierce wind was the most amazing moment of my life. Moses must have felt the same way because he began to sing about it all. I couldn't help joining in with a little song of my own, dancing as we went along.

Of course, it wasn't all like that. We trudged through the desert for years. God provided food, but we missed the juicy cucumbers and mouth-watering fruits we could get in Egypt. I got a bit jealous too, of how close Moses was to his wife Zipporah, his children and father-in-law Jethro who had all come with him from Midian. I grumbled to Moses that he shouldn't have married foreigners. God was so cross with me that he sent an awful skin disease to plague me. Moses pleaded with God and I was forgiven and healed. I tried to make friends with them after that as we all needed to support one another in the hard days in the desert.

As I finished, there was silence for a minute, then Isla, the thoughtful one in the class spoke up,

"She wasn't right all the time ,sir, was she?

"No, all the Bible heroes got things wrong almost as often as they got things right. That's one of the reasons people believe the stories. We know nobody is perfect. Now, off you go, see you next week."

CHAPTER TWO: GIVE ME THIS MOUNTAIN

"Wayne, that could only be described as loitering."

"Sir?" came the puzzled reply.

With a sigh Zac spelled it out for him.

"You should already be in class yet here you are, hanging around at the other end of the corridor, obviously up to no good. Explain."

"Sir, please sir, I wanted to catch you before tomorrow. Will you tell us another story, and can it be someone we've never heard of before?"

That made Zak laugh and he agreed but sent Wayne packing before someone else caught him. He would be in enough trouble being late for class. Strolling into his office Zac sighed again at the mountain of paperwork waiting for him. Sometimes he wondered if he had done the right thing going for promotion to Deputy Head. It was the teaching itself he really enjoyed and did so little of nowadays. Resigned to the inevitable, he dragged out a pile of dull looking documents from County

Hall and prepared for a boring couple of hours. Just before he got started, Zac wondered about the request for another hero story. Then it dawned on him. The obvious one to go for was one of his favourites and it would follow on naturally from Miriam. Smiling to himself , he settled to work…

They shut down the laptops, the piece of research on Hindu gods completed, and looked at Zak eagerly, waiting for a new story.

oOo

"Caleb. Leave that to someone else, we've got to go," shouted my friend Joshua.

I looked down pointedly at my bare foot. I was repairing a broken sandal strap of my own. Remarking that whatever it was would just have to wait, I put in the last few stitches and slipped the sandal onto my foot. Then we ran to join the other few folks gathered in front of Moses. Glares greeted us as we had obviously kept everyone waiting. Even though Joshua and I were leaders in our own tribes I grew uneasy when I recognised the others as older and more important.

"Why are we here?" I whispered to Joshua.

"Shh" came from the folks around us as Moses had already begun speaking.

He explained that just over the next line of hills was the country that God had promised would be our very own homeland. We needed information as to what we were facing before we led the people into new territory. We were being sent to gather that information. One from each of the tribes had been chosen for their abilities to move stealthily and quickly. Moses explained what he needed to know,

"Take note of the people. Do they seem weak or strong? Are there many of them? Are their cities just camps or do they have fortified strongholds? Look at the land. Is it fertile? You need to bring back samples of what it can produce. Oh, and take note of what forests there are as we shall need wood in large quantities."

We were sent to equip ourselves. I waited near Joshua's tent when I was ready and we set off together. There were a few reasonable tracks through the hills and most of us took off in the same direction. It was exciting to be the first to see what might prove to be our new home and we took careful note of everything, spreading out to cover as much ground as possible. Eventually, Joshua and I met up again with our samples of the grain and fruit as well as twigs for Moses to see what trees there were.

Some of the others had brought the biggest bunch of grapes I had ever seen. It was so heavy they had threaded it on a pole so two of them could help each other to carry it! One way or another, our arrival back at camp created quite a stir and a crowd soon gathered to listen as we reported back to Moses.

We let the older ones from the other tribes speak first and they told of how it was indeed a land flowing with milk and honey just as God had promised. Wonderful after the barren desert. But wait! I couldn't believe what I heard next! Yes, true there were fortified cities and the people were tall and strong like they said, but saying we were like grasshoppers at the side of them…really?

I couldn't help it. I had to butt in.

"Look, we can do it. Let's go in at once. We'll manage, you'll see.

There was instant uproar. No matter what Joshua and I said, they wouldn't listen. They even started coming out with things like,

"We were better off in Egypt."

"Let's choose another leader and go back there."

I was horrified and Joshua and I both tore our robes in the age old sign for our people that we were mourning a great tragedy. We tried to get them to trust God and explained that if we did not rebel and He was pleased with us He would help us and give us the land as he had promised. It was no good. Then we sensed that God Himself had come to the tent of meeting so we made ourselves scarce and left Moses to talk to Him about our situation.

We found out later that God was so disgusted with His people that He did not want them anymore and offered to make a new nation from Moses family instead. Moses pleaded for us all and eventually it was agreed that God would keep us. However, the rebels were not to enter our new land . Instead we were all to wander the desert until their generation died of old age. Only Joshua and I were to survive as we had believed.

Zac stood up.

"That's it for today. Time to pack away."

"Aw, sir, we want to know what happens next."

"What happens next is I give you your homework."

Amid mutters and grumbles, Zac brought out a tray of get well cards.

"You are all to take one of these and write an encouraging message for Miss Morris. She is very ill with cancer and won't be coming back this year. Bring them to my room at break tomorrow."

Isla wanted to know why he had called it RE homework so Zac explained that learning to think of others was part of religious education. Subdued, they collected the cards on the way out.

There was one left. Staring at it he decided he had better learn his own lesson and took that one to write on himself.

To Zac's surprise every single one of the cards was brought back. He itched to steam them open and read what they considered was encouragement but thought it was unethical. Besides, it was sure to be obvious what he had done. Perhaps Angie would show them to him later.

She answered the door in an old fleece robe, with eyes red-rimmed from crying. Awkwardly he offered to come back another time and thrust the cards into her hands. She opened the door wider and said,

"Come in. I would offer you a cup of coffee but there aren't any clean cups."

Glancing at the state of the sink at the kitchen end of the long through lounge, he guessed she was right. He encouraged her to sit and look at the cards. Taking his jacket off, he washed up and made them both some coffee. There was half a packet of chocolate biscuits in the cupboard and when he brought it all to Ange, she cried again. He rummaged in all the clutter until he found a box of tissues and passed them to her. Soon she was composed enough to eat a couple of biscuits and drink the coffee. She even smiled when she passed a few of the funniest cards to him to look at.

Predictably, Big Dave showed his usual lack of tact. After the usual get well wish he had said not to rush back because Mr Johnson was telling some good stories. Hastily Zak told her about the bribe he was using to get them to cooperate. Angie sniffed into her tissue and said,

"Good for you. I'm not cut out for teaching. If I could think of something else to do I would."

Hastily Zac picked another one out and laughed again. Wayne was offering his Mum's purple disco wig if she needed it as,

"Me mum don't go out no more since she got all of us."

One moved both of them. It was from Isla, talking about her big sister having cancer. She reassured Ange that the Macmillan nurses helped a lot. Zak urged her to follow up on Isla's idea. He also said,

"Have you got family who can help?

She shook her head. The family were estranged and had lost touch. Some cousins lived near Cardiff but she did not know them very well. He found himself asking for a shopping list and offering to come back the next day.

At the next lesson with 5JR he told them how touched Miss Morris had been by the cards, but NOT how many times he had been back since. Finishing the lesson purposefully early, he took up the threads of the story.

oOo

Making camp for the night I noticed that the hills ahead of us looked familiar. Excitedly, I went towards the leader's tent. Moses was dead. The whole of that generation was already gone. Joshua and I were the only two left, thanks to us both believing that what God had said was true. Joshua was now our leader. Both of us were still as tough and fit at eighty years old as we had been at forty when we had spied out the land. I told Joshua we had arrived. Our initial excitement was dampened a little when we thought of what awaited us, especially the river Jordan. To get to where we were supposed to go, it would have to be crossed just at the time of year when it was in full flood. Apparently God had told Joshua how it would be done for he was soon organising everyone into a line leading to the edge of the water with the Levites leading the way carrying the box on poles that had God's commandments to us inside it, carved onto pieces of stone.

As soon as they stepped into the water, God caused a dry path to open up. He had said that one person from each tribe should carry a big stone and to pile them up in the middle. We were a fickle lot , so a sight of the cairn in the dry season would remind everyone what God had done for them. We agreed to help one another subdue each area before finally settling on our own lands.

The territory had already been portioned out to the tribes. Finally we reached my area. As I knew the Lord would help me subdue the giants, the descendants of

Anak, I had asked for the mountainous region. I hoped this would calm the fears of the others and encourage them to move into the land God had given them.

That seemed a good idea at the time, but now, in the half-light before dawn, peering up the steep and slippery slope at the stronghold above us, I wasn't so sure. Praying that God would show us what to do, I thought hard. They would expect us to attack from here as we knew the slope in the rear of the fortress was even steeper. What if we were to do the unexpected and go that way? All of us were fit so it might be possible. I separated out a contingent to come with me, while the rest I told to make noisy preparations to attack, but to wait for those who fled down the slope.

We made it! The final stretch was a struggle as we needed to keep as quiet as possible. We could hear the fighting now, so we scaled the unguarded back wall and using all the cover we could find we crept up on the warriors hurling rocks and spears down at the rest of my army. Our swords took out many before they knew what was happening but then they turned to fight us. They were huge! Quickly, before anyone had time to feel paralysed by fear, I gave a blood-curdling yell and led the attack.

What we lacked in stature we made up for in skill and ferocity and they were soon overcome. The rest of the troops at the foot of the slope picked off the ones who decided to flee and the place was ours. Bit by bit we subdued the whole region until only one stronghold remained. I had an idea to boost the flagging spirits of the men who had been fighting hard for so long. My daughter Achsah was ready to marry and settle down, so we hit on a plan to find someone who really trusted God and would be a good protector for her. I challenged the young warriors to devise a way to take the city of Kiriath- Sepher and said what I had a mind to do with regards to my daughter.

Her cousin, Othniel must have really cared about her as he went all out to take the stronghold and breached its defences first. They were married, and as a wedding gift I gave her a field with springs of good, clear water to help them to set up there.

We took all the land we had been allocated but not everyone did as well as us. Some enemies were not driven out and those groups continued to make trouble. But it was wonderful that we now had a land of our own.

To Zac's secret embarrassment, fervent applause greeted the end of the story. In the silence that followed Isla said thoughtfully,

"Sir it wasn't being a good warrior that made Caleb a hero, was it?"

"No, it was his unshakable faith that God could do anything if people trusted Him to act for them. That is still the same today for anyone who decides to rely on God. Now, this sheet has your homework on it. See you next week."

CHAPTER THREE: MIGHTY WARRIOR? YOU MUST BE JOKING!

Zac stretched and massaged the back of his neck. His fit watch beeped and a seated figure appeared on it. Hmm. He had been sitting for far too long but you can't mark work while exercising. He needed to get out for a bit. With the longer summer days it was still light outside and he began a slow jog along the still busy street. The corner shop was still open so he made a detour to buy some apples and set off again. He began to go faster now he was warmed up and arrived breathless and hot at Angie's door.

Giving a shout to warn her who it was, he let himself in. Stretched out on the sofa she was watching an old repeat of "Who wants to be a millionaire?" He enjoyed it too so he pulled up a chair and tossed her the apples as he began munching one himself. They shouted out answers, comfortable in each other's company. As it ended she switched off and said she had to be up early to

go for a scan the next day . It was Saturday so he offered
to take her.

It went according to plan at the hospital, with only a
short wait before it was her turn. As he dropped her at
home Angie said she would text him when she got the
results. The following week went fast and soon it was time
for 5JR's RE lesson again. He had a good idea for another
story and timed the lesson to end a bit earlier to give him
chance to start it before home time.

oOo

We traipsed into the farmhouse as dawn was
breaking, heaving the full sacks in with us. It was no joke
trying to harvest the grain on a night with very little
moonlight. Too easy to cut someone's toes off-or your
own. But if we had left it much longer the enemy army
would have fetched it and probably torched the farm
afterwards. Many of the farms had lost their harvests
already in the raids from Midian and it was only a matter of
time until they reached us. They were like swarms of
locusts taking everything they found. No, worse. Locusts

ate crops but these monsters took the herds of cattle as well.

My little sister was crying. Funny how small children pick up on a tense atmosphere but I had something for her. Taking them out of my pouch very carefully, I gave her the few chamzitz plants I had found while we were harvesting. I knew she loved the flavour. She waved them at my mother and said,

"Look, Imma, Gid'on brought these."

They went off to wash the sorrel- like stems while my father drew me to one side,

"Gid'on, I need you to start threshing this grain."

"But Abba, the soldiers will see me and just come and take it from us."

"I've thought of that. Your brothers have taken some to the pit we use as a winepress. The chaff won't blow as far as the top of the pit so the dust won't be seen to give you away."

That seemed reasonable and I wanted us to have it processed into flour and hidden as soon as possible. Wolfing down some bread and hard cheese as I went, I made for the steep stone steps leading down to the large area we used to process the grapes. It was deep enough to hide even my taller than average height so I felt reasonably safe. Even so, I did not work under the shade of the terebinth tree on the far side of the pit but I stayed near the steps so no one could sneak up on me.

Already tired, I wished we could have brought the oxen down the steps to tread the grain as they usually did when we worked on the proper threshing floor. It took me a while to find the right rhythm of the flail, lifting it overhead and banging down the free end attached with leather to the wood in my hand. Soon, the pile of grains had their husks split open and I began winnowing the dust and chaff before I put the usable kernels of wheat into the now empty sacks. Idly I wondered why Midian had turned against us. After all, Moses wife was the daughter of the priest of Midian so we must have been friends once.

On the edge of my awareness I noticed a figure under the tree. That really spooked me as no one had come past me down the steps. Was it a Midianite spy? I was just thinking about running up the steps to fetch my brothers when the figure spoke to me. He said the craziest thing,

"The Lord is with you, mighty and brave man."

I couldn't help it. The bitter and sarcastic reply just poured out of me,

"If He *is* with us why has he left us alone to face the Midian army? There is scarcely an untouched farm in the land."

"*That* is why I am sending you to save your people."

Dumfounded, I sank down on the steps behind me whimpering,

"Why me? How can I possibly do that? I am the weakest of our household and our family holds no importance in our clan."

Holding my eyes with his compelling gaze I was told that He would be with me and I would defeat the Midianite army as if it were just one man.

My thoughts and heart both racing I felt as if I needed some kind of reassurance before committing myself to this crazy plan. So, I asked that if He really *was* The Lord, would he wait there while I prepared an offering for him. When he agreed and settled down under the tree to wait, I ran up the steps to prepare meat from a goat kid, and a bowl of broth. Part of me hoped he had gone, but no, he rose from under the tree to greet me, bidding me set the food on a handy flat rock.

Imagine how I felt when he touched his staff to the food and fire consumed the lot as he vanished from sight. Whoa, this must really have been the Angel of the Lord. I collapsed to my knees in fear. Reassurance flooded me that I was accepted so I built an altar there and then. I Seemed to hear that what our God wanted was the altar to false gods in the city torn down and a proper one to Him should be built and I was the one to do it. I was to use the family's second best bull to get meat for the sacrifice.

I trembled inside as I realised how truly stuffed I was. The city folk would kill me if I did what God wanted me to do, but did I really want to risk God being angry with me for disobeying? Thinking furiously, I decided there was a way it might be done. Taking the sacks of grain one by one to be made into flour, I went back into the farmhouse to catch up on some sleep and then after nightfall I would put my plan into action.

oOo

There were a few moans as Zak drew the lesson to a close but they began to drift off down the corridor. As soon as the last two or three were out of earshot, Zak drew his phone from his pocket. It had stopped vibrating but he rang Angie back and she answered at once. She was calm but he could hear the upset in her voice. The scan had shown more growth in the cancer and they had scheduled an operation for her in a fortnight. Zak said,

"Look, I've got about an hour and a half here on paperwork, why don't I bring a takeaway round for us?" She agreed but it was nearer to two hours before he

managed to clear up all the statistics the Head had wanted. He found Bob, the caretaker, strolling down the corridor to see if he had finished as he wanted to lock up.

The meal with Angie wasn't fun precisely, but she relaxed as the evening went on. She was resigned to the idea of more surgery and even managed to laugh a little as they watched the umpteenth re-run of "Only fools and Horses" together. Back at his flat, he looked round it with fresh eyes. It seemed soulless and sterile. Even while Angie was ill she was managing to put a little colour and life into her surroundings.

By the time he saw 5JR again on the Thursday before half term, he was ready to complete Gideon's story.

oOo

Ten of my servants came with me and we sneaked to the city. It did not take us long to pull apart the ramshackle heap of rocks they used as an altar. Then it was just a matter of choosing the twelve largest stones to represent our twelve tribes and setting them into place. We had brought wood with us for the fire on top. The bull we had already carved into joints carried in sacks so it would be easier to hoist onto the altar. Picking up our things we ran as soon as the wood was alight before the flames and smoke woke everyone up. Luckily the track was very stony so it would be hard to follow our trail. We crept to our beds to sleep away what remained of the night.

Unfortunately, someone managed to work out who had torn down the city altar because I was woken by the shouts of a mob at the door and my father shouting back. Quickly, I dragged on a clean robe and rushed through the house. As I walked up behind him they were demanding that I be brought out to be put to death. My father's quick wits saved the day. He yelled out,

"It's a poor sort of god who needs defending by you. If he has any power surely he will strike down my son. If not, perhaps Gideon is right to show us a better way."

After standing and watching for a while they eventually moved off, back to the city. Probably disappointed not to see me bitten by a snake or struck by lightning.

A few days of peace ended when vast hordes from Midian crossed the river from the east and camped in the next valley. It was our turn to face the raiders. True to His word God inspired me with His Spirit to call together the men of the land. Weary of being dispirited and defeated they answered the call in their thousands.

Afraid and unsure of myself still, I decided to check with God that it really was me who was meant to save the country. Perhaps I could ask for some kind of sign. Finally I hit on the idea of putting a fleece from the sheep onto the threshing floor. If God could use me, I asked him to cause the fleece to be wet with dew the next morning but the rest of the floor to be dry.

And that is exactly what I found. With a sinking feeling I realised that saving the land was to be my job. Of course, it could be a coincidence so very apologetically I asked if the sign could be given again the following night, but the other way round. It wasn't much of a surprise to find a dry fleece on a very wet floor. Oh dear... Resigned to my fate, I led the huge crowd of tribesmen who had answered the call to camp just south of where the army from Midian had now settled in.

God didn't seem pleased with the size of our army. Admittedly it was smaller than the ones ranged against us. But no, that wasn't the problem. God seemed to think that if we won with all the folk we had, we might begin to think how powerful we were and forget to serve and worship Him once again. That was how all this trouble started in the first place! So, He said He would show me how to cut down the size of the army to what He would use.

Still, it made a kind of sense so I passed on God's instructions to send home all who were so afraid of the coming battle that they were trembling with fear. I felt like joining them but the thought of our amazing God fighting for us stopped me. Still, when twenty-two thousand sloped off I was more than a little worried. God told me that was still too many. He got me to get them to go to the water of the spring to get a drink as it was very hot. Anyone who flung himself flat to lap like a dog was to be sent home. The ones who remained cautious and aware of their surroundings by cupping water in their hands could stay.

Horrified, I watched as only three hundred out of the ten thousand soldiers used their hands and the rest were sent home. The rest of us regarded one another with dismay.

As it got dark God told me we could attack anytime but only in the way He would tell us. If I was still afraid I should go to the Midianite camp first and listen in. Purah, the servant who had cared for me for so long insisted on going with me and we inched our way to the edge of the rocks overhanging their camp just as the watch was being set. A few of them were settling in for the night and as we listened one of them described an unsettling dream he couldn't forget.

"This great loaf of barley bread rolled into camp demolishing the tents."

In the silence that followed, another of them spoke up,

"That stands for Gideon. I am sure he will defeat us when he comes."

Murmurs of fear gave way to silence as they drifted off to sleep. We took the opportunity to slip away back to our camp. My heart was full of worship as I realised God had primed the enemy for defeat.

Quickly we finished our preparations. Each of the three hundred were given burning torches hidden in pottery jars, and a trumpet. They were split into three groups of a hundred to make their way around the outside of the sleeping camp. At my signal they blew the trumpets as I shouted,

"For the Lord and for Gideon!"

There was even more noise as we smashed the jars and the light of the torches blazed out while we shouted,

"A sword for the Lord and for Gideon!"

Trumpets were slung round our necks and swords were drawn but we needn't have bothered. Eyes blinded by the torches and confused after waking from sleep they couldn't make out how few of us there were. In their panic and confusion they hacked at anybody who came near them, killing each other as they took flight and raced back to the borders to get to the safety of their own country.

That turned out to be exactly the wrong thing to do. Many of our tribes who had lost crops and animals seized the opportunity to right a few wrongs. Few of the Midianites reached the border and their leaders were taken and killed.

Oh yes, we were so grateful at first and enjoyed our peaceful life as farmers once more. As the years rolled by, though, I was sure that our people would slip back into their old ways and forget what we owed to God.

oOo

Big Dave blurted out,

"Huh! You can't call him a hero. He was scared all the time."

That was just the opening Zak wanted and he began to explain that it was acting in spite of his fears that made him a real hero. Any mindless fool could blunder on and conquer almost by accident. Gideon relied on God to help him get through the tough times and we could too. Just then the bell went. While everyone was on the move, Isla's friend Summer shouted,

"Have a good half-term, Sir. What about a heroine next time?"

"We'll see…"

Summer chipped back,

"My Mum says that when she means no, but she doesn't want to start an argument."

Zak laughed. He remembered his own Mum doing the same thing. Well, perhaps he could find a good story with a brave woman in it. He left to put the finishing touches to preparations for the In-Service Training Day booked in for tomorrow. Boring. Some bright young thing saying why all their tried and trusted techniques should be changed. Ah well. At least there was the prospect of a week off.

CHAPTER FOUR: FOR SUCH A TIME AS THIS

It seemed all wrong to be getting up at 5am in the holiday. Zak yawned and somehow made it through the daily rituals of dressing and breakfast. Checking he had his wallet he locked the door and drove blearily through the empty streets to Angie's. He helped her double check that she had what she needed and that the flat was clean and tidy then they were off, mostly silent with gloomy thoughts. Before 7am they were being ushered into a little side room in the hospital and the first of many tests and checks had begun.

Angie shivered. Zak suspected it was from fear more than cold.

"You're in a good hospital," he whispered, "there are some amazing surgeons here."

Even when the next nurse came in he kept hold of her hand and gave it a squeeze. As she was measured for surgical stockings he assured her he would be praying for her and left before he broke down. Unshed tears blurred his vision and he bumped into an empty wheelchair which had been left in the corridor.

The day seemed endless. At 8pm he gave in and rang the ward. He was relieved to find that the operation had gone well and she was "comfortable" which he suspected was bending the truth. Visitors were not allowed until Thursday and by then he was so anxious that he arrived half an hour too soon and ended up having to wait ages in the corridor as visiting times were strict.

When he found her at the end of the ward, she looked so pale he almost broke down again. One arm was out of action so he opened his card and held it for her to read, then opened the neatly wrapped parcel (done by the shop). He had decided flowers were a nuisance for the nurses and she may not be allowed chocolates so he had settled for a finely knitted shawl in shades and patterns of moss and heather. She exclaimed in delight as he put it round her shoulders. With the draught from the open window he realised it had been a good choice.

Zak visited every day. The social worker decided that with living alone she could not really go home so a place was found for her in a local nursing home for two weeks. He brought in extra clothes for her but could not stay as half term was over and he had a staff meeting. 5JR had heard about Angie's operation and some had brought cards to class with them and asked if Sir could deliver them. He agreed he might be able to do that and they left them on his desk. Towards the end of the lesson he began the next story:

oOo

"Auntie…"

"No, only your Mum is English, so we call her auntie. I am your Jewish Abba's sister so you call me Mume."

Sarah was far too excited to take it all in. It was the first time they had all celebrated Purim and Mume Karmia had come to help them get ready. She helped them dress in the costumes she had made. David had opted for his namesake, David, of Goliath slaying fame, but Sarah wanted to be the star of the show, so she put on a floaty purple dress and crown to be Esther. While the adults got ready, freshly made Hamentaschen (Haman's pockets) were given them: delicious three cornered, open pastry cups stuffed full with chocolate or seeds or fruit or nuts.

Mume Karmia passed each of them a grogger, a kind of wooden rattle, to blot out the villain's name when they heard it in the story. Their mother stayed behind to prepare the special meal but the rest of them were soon in the synagogue ready to listen to the Megillah, the book of Esther, telling how the Jewish people had been saved.

They heard of the little girl Esther, who was orphaned when only tiny but had been brought up by her older cousin Mordecai as part of his household. (Each time they were mentioned in the story people were encouraged to cheer. It reminded Sarah of the pantomime they had been to just after Christmas.) It all took place during the time that the Jewish people had been taken away captive into Babylon. The court of the Kingdom travelled around four cities in turn and the events written up in The Megillah happened when King Ahasuerus and his followers were in Susa and Esther was a young woman.

The King gave a great party for all the important generals and princes. For six months the festivities went on while his Queen, Vashti, held her own celebrations for all the women. The king decided to show off his wife and commanded her to come out and show herself to all the men. She thought this was a terrible idea and refused. His counsellors, probably as drunk as the king was, urged him to remove her as queen and send out messengers through the kingdom to look for young women to replace her.

Mordecai told Esther (tentative cheers and they were all encouraged to shout louder) to go along but to keep her nationality secret. When she captivated the king, she was chosen as the new queen. Mordecai (loud shouts) got a job as a palace gatekeeper so he could be on hand to help if things went wrong. Standing there on guard, he was unnoticed by two plotters finalising a plan to kill the king. Mordecai reported it and they were dealt with, while Mordecai's prompt action was written into the court records.

It was about this time that the king promoted a man called Haman (Boos, hisses and loud rattles from the groggers) to be in charge of all the kings officials. Unfortunately he was the kind of self- important person who let it go to his head. He insisted that as he passed by everyone should bow down to him. (More boos.) Only Mordecai stood straight at attention instead of bowing.(Loud cheers). Haman (Boo, rattle) got angrier each time this happened, finally making enquiries about this impudent rascal. On learning that he was one of the captured Jews he resolved to kill ALL of them, not just Mordecai and plotted how best it could be done. With the aid of a very large donation to the king's treasury he obtained Ahasuerus' permission for his plans to kill off this rebellious group.

oOo

Zak shuffled the work on his desk into a pile and told them they would have to wait a week for the rest of the story. He was unmoved by the various whines and groans and followed them out. Dropping the work on his office desk he hurried outside. One of the perks of his new job was that he didn't normally supervise the mass exodus onto the buses but he was filling in for a junior member of staff who had gone home ill. Two fights and a spitting episode later, they were all safely ushered onto the correct vehicles and he could head back in out of the rain. It took about an hour to clear the backlog of paperwork and then he was off, driving to Angie's nursing home.

She was already packed up and eager to get back to her own little flat. They stopped off on the way to get groceries but they were soon eating the quick pasta meal Zak cooked for them both. Checking that she could manage, Zak left as soon as he had washed the dishes. She followed him to the door to thank him with a little kiss on the cheek. He promised to pop in at the weekend, and after explaining that the evenings would be taken up with planning next year's very complex timetable, he left, saying,

"Text me if you need anything and I will get it to you somehow."

She did send a text but only to let him know that a friend from college days was staying with her for the rest of the week so he relaxed a bit knowing she would have some help. Some of the timetable had to be re-done as the young member of staff who had gone home ill announced she was pregnant and would be unavailable from September. Luckily, they were interviewing college students for a first probationary post so one of them might be able to fill the gap. He was more than a little distracted in his only class that day, but 5JR were on their best behaviour as they wanted the rest of the story from last week.

oOo

Haman (boo, hiss) and his cronies cast Pur (casting lots) to decide the most auspicious day for their awful deed. The thirteenth day of Adar, the twelfth Jewish month was picked and the decree sent out by the very efficient Babylonian messenger system. It stated that on that day all the Jews were to be killed and all their belongings were to be plundered.

When Mordecai heard what was planned he put on the traditional mourning garb, draping himself in sackcloth and covering his head and face with ashes. One of the servants told Esther about Mordecai and wondering who they knew had died she sent someone to ask him. He sent back a written copy of the decree and begged her to intercede for them with the king. Esther, dismayed, sent back that even as Queen she could not go into the King's private apartments to speak with him unless he had sent for her. Anyone doing so was suspected of seeking to kill the king and was arrested and put to death.

Mordecai sent back the uncompromising message,

"Do not think you will escape this decree just because you are in the palace. If you fail us, the Jews will have help from somewhere, but it will surely be the end of you. After all, who knows, perhaps you have received your special place in the Kingdom for such a time as this."

After deep thought, Esther sent back the reply,

"If you and all the Jews in Susa go without food for three days, I and my maids will also fast and then I will try to see the king even though it is against the law, and if I perish, I perish."

At the end of the three days she went to the door of the inner court where the king noticed her. What would he do? Mume Karmia and the children joined in the shouts exhorting the king to save her. Yes, it was all right, he was captivated anew by her and held out his royal sceptre, the symbol of his power, and she was able to go into the throne room. In fact Ahasuerus was so besotted that he offered her anything she liked, up to half his kingdom. Mysteriously she would not tell him there and then but said she would prepare a banquet for the King and his chief advisor, Haman (BOO, rattle) on the following day. Intrigued he agreed.

Of course, Haman (rattle rattle) was even more puffed up and boasted about the dinner with the Queen to anyone who would listen, especially his longsuffering wife.

He grumbled that it was all spoiled when he saw that wretch, Mordecai (CHEERS) still refusing to bow down to him.

"Have him hanged," suggested his wife, callously.

What a fine idea, and they soon had the gallows erected for the following day, sure that the king would grant permission.

However, that night the king could not sleep and thinking what would be boring enough to help him doze off he sent for the annals (diaries) of the court. Far from going to sleep he seemed to be wider awake than ever by the time he reached the fairly recent entries. Here, he read of a plot against his life and how it had been foiled by the vigilance of the gatekeeper. Aware that he owed his life to this man he asked what reward had been given to him. The tired guards looked at each other and shrugged, chorusing

"Nothing, Sire."

Ahasuerus thought for a moment, then said,

"See if there is anyone in the outer court who we can ask to help."

They returned moments later with Haman (rattle, boo) who had been waiting to ask permission for the hanging he planned. He swept an elaborate bow and waited to see what the king required. Ahasuerus asked,

"What should be done for the man that the king delights to honour?"

In his vanity, Haman (Loud boos and rattles) decided that must mean himself so he suggested,

"Oh, parade him round the city in royal robes and a crown on one of the king's own horses. Someone ought to go with him to cry out about you honouring this man.

Ahasuerus thought this a splendid idea and had one of the crowns and a robe fetched straight away. He passed them to Haman (rattle) but as he was about to put them on, to his chagrin and dismay he heard the instructions that he was to parade Mordecai (Loud cheers) around the city. Aaaah! Later, creeping back home a broken man, he told his wife all that had happened. She said,

"If this Mordecai (applause and cheers) is of the Jewish people, you will not prevail against him."

Haman (rattle) just had time to change before servants came to fetch him to Esther's banquet.(loud cheers)

oOo

And you will have to wait till next week for the final part of the story. As they all packed up and left, Samia lingered and Zak noticed her fearful look at the door. When he asked what the matter was, she said,

"Vicky and Ann are picking on me." Puzzled Zak said,

"But I thought you were all best mates?"

She explained that they wouldn't have anything to do with her ever since she refused to go drinking in the park with them.

"Huh! They aren't very good friends if they try to make you do something that's wrong. What about Eve, I've noticed they aren't very nice to her. Don't you both go to

the same youth club? Perhaps you might be able to help each other?"

"Thanks, sir. I'll see her there tonight."

She went off looking more cheerful leaving Zak to ponder what he had learned. How had the girl got hold of the booze? He knew Vicky's older brother had just gone to prison for drug dealing and wondered if she was heading the same way. Perhaps the social worker, Val Jessop should look into this. He might have to bring the parents in.

Later he asked Angie what she thought. She had heard that Ann's dad had gone off with another woman, leaving her Mum to cope with four children on her own. No wonder the pair had teamed up. Definitely had grudges against the world. He would have to see if he could help before major problems set in. Then they settled in for a bit of escapist fun with a corny old film.

It was getting closer to the end of the summer term so he and Val Jessop got to work on the family problems of the two girls straight away. They put in several home *visits, alerted various official bodies, got some financial help for Ann's mum and explained to the two girls about the risks their drinking could bring. As well as damaging their health, if they got drunk, they were vulnerable to attack and abuse. They had apparently stolen the drink in the corner shop. Their mums dragged them along to apologise and pay for it, making them promise never to do it again. On Zak's advice they were given a small amount of pocket money on the understanding it would be increased if they could stay out of trouble for the next six months. He also alerted their next year's teacher to keep a close eye on them.*

One week of 5JR's lesson had been missed because of a school trip, so it was a fortnight later when he got to teach them again. He was pleased to see that Samia and Eve had come in together giggling, and were also chatting to Vicky and Ann. He got them settled and the lesson went well, stopping in time to finish off the story.

oOo

Esther's banquet lasted two full days and as they were nearing the end Ahasuerus said to tell them what her request was, again promising anything up to half his kingdom for her. At last she spoke up,

"I am begging you for my life and the lives of all my people. If we were just to be sold as slaves I would have kept silent, but there is a plot to kill us all and that would be a great loss to you my king."

"Who dares to plot against you?"

"A foe and an enemy…this wicked Haman." (Sarah and David joined in the great shout against him) He cowered down in terror before the king.

Ahasuerus was beside himself with anger and strode out into Esther's garden to compose himself. Haman stayed to plead with Esther. (All those in the synagogue were now jeering and shouting so it was a few moments before the story could continue.) Just as the miserable wretch threw himself onto the couch beside her, the king returned and jumped to the conclusion that this was an assault.

Guards told the king of the high gallows Haman had prepared to hang Mordecai so it seemed fitting that they should be used to hang Haman himself and he was led away. (A final burst of sound from the groggers.) Esther admitted at last that she was cousin to Mordecai and that she had been brought up by him. He was sent for and was given Lordship over all Haman's household and his riches. At the same time, Mordecai was placed in authority and given the king's ring, to seal documents in the king's name.

However it was too soon for sighs of relief as the King explained that once a decree went out, according to the law it could not be repealed. They thought deeply about how the massacre could be averted. Mordecai was given the authority to think up a plan and send out his own decree in the king's name, sealed with the official ring he had been given. He finally decided to write that on the thirteenth day of Adar the Jews were allowed to gather together and defend themselves against all attacks.

Mordecai was given royal robes and a crown and there was great rejoicing. (Sarah and David joined in all the deafening cheers.) People were afraid of the Jews and some even pretended to be Jewish. When the day of the attack finally came, the Jews defended themselves and no one could stand against them. From that time on, the Feast of Purim, or Lots, had been commemorated on the fourteenth day of Adar. Gifts were given and food shared with the poor.

Sarah and David clapped and cheered with the rest and took forward their baskets of food to put with the other gifts for distribution to those in need. Then they hurried home with Abba and Mume Karmia to share the feast and presents which Imma had waiting for them.

oOo

Zak leaned back and reached for the bottle of water on his desk. As he soothed his parched throat, Isla said,

"Sir it was just like Hitler wasn't it?"

Before he could agree, Big Dave chimed in,

"What you on about?"

Curious to see what she would say, Zak kept quiet and let Isla answer.

"Well, he tried to get rid of the Jews in the second world war but he didn't manage it and he lost didn't he Sir."

"Exactly."

Ann sighed. Esther was very brave, risking her life like that. I don't think I could be a hero."

"No," replied Zak, "nor me. But luckily most of us don't have to cope with life or death situations. Sometimes though, it takes a lot of bravery just standing up for what is right when everyone else is trying to persuade us to do wrong."

He noticed Ann, Vicki, Samia and Eve share glances and smiles just before Samia said,

"Sir, did Esther's people ever get back to their own country?"

"Not all of them wanted to leave, but yes, some did. That reminds me of another hero I could tell you about. Now, it's time to go home.

CHAPTER FIVE: FACING OPPOSITION

"Sir, we've finished listing the websites for our homework, can't we have the next story now?"

The clamour of yes and please died down as Zak shot them all a quelling look. After explaining that the next superhero was still in Susa but about twenty years later than Esther and Mordecai, Zak began this particular favourite of his.

The news from home was not good. Hanani, my brother had travelled (from those left in Jerusalem) to see me. When I asked how the ones left behind were getting on, he paused for a moment sipping his wine, but after gathering his thoughts he replied,

"Nehemiah, they are in great trouble. The walls around Jerusalem which protected them so well are broken down and the huge wooden gates were smashed and burned. Attacks come from the wild tribes on every side."

I wept for them but could not see how to help so I fasted and prayed for days. It was probably only what we deserved for how badly we had betrayed and ignored God, so I told Him that as I prayed. But I reminded Him we were still His people and begged for his help. All this left me in a turmoil as I went about my job. Did I mention I was cupbearer to the King? He noticed how upset I was, as I passed him his wine after tasting it. He commented and I was terrified in case he thought I was plotting against him. There was nothing else for it, he had to be told the whole sorry tale.

Zak paused to explain that King Artaxerxes was probably the son of Ahasuerus who was also known as Xerxes and he may well have been Esther's son also.

The king listened intently while I described what had happened to Jerusalem and then asked what my request was. Taking a moment for a swift prayer for help, I asked to be allowed to go back home and rebuild the city. I think the Queen beside him may have encouraged him to care about their ancestral home for he sanctioned the trip and even gave me letters for safe passage through the various provinces. There was also a letter to Asaph, the keeper of the King's forests, with instructions to provide the timber we would need for the gates. And so we set off. I was given an escort of soldiers from the king's army. Probably just as well when I thought of all the attacks on Jerusalem.

oOo

We ran out of time at that point. None of the class lingered as it was the night of the upper forms' disco. Zak rushed off as well, being the obligatory senior member of staff for the night (otherwise known as, "the lamb to the slaughter"). The head would welcome everyone at 7pm and after half an hour she would disappear and leave the rest to Zak. The caretaker and he would see everyone off the premises then clear up and lock up. Happy days. At least he needn't get there till about twenty past seven. Angie said she felt well enough to cook, so Zak headed there straight away. His trendy (NOT) gear for the disco was in the car already so he needn't go home at all.

The lasagne and salad was lovely, with a smashing homemade apple pie to finish off. Good job he was policing the gig rather than dancing. One or two younger members of staff would be there to dance and mingle. Zak bagged the bathroom to freshen up and change, then headed for the door. Angie followed and looked him up and down.

"Not sure the jacket and jeans really suit the occasion, but you might at least get the tie straight."

She stepped close to adjust it and Zak gave in to temptation and did what he had dreamed of doing for a while...leaned in and gave her a lingering kiss on the lips. For a moment she responded and then a horrified look crossed her face and she whisked herself inside and shut the door.

Ruefully he figured that during the last couple of years without a girlfriend he must have lost his touch. He never used to have that effect! The rest of the evening went off well. In assembly the following morning it was announced that £1,156.04 had been raised towards the fund for more IT equipment and the head announced a competition for the best ideas for future fundraising. As she also announced prizes of tokens for Amazon, that caused quite a buzz.

After school Zak picked up a takeaway and rather apprehensively knocked on Angie's door. She did not look exactly welcoming but let him in and got dishes and hot drinks in silence. After a rather uneasy meal , he said bluntly,

"What gives?"

"I.." she fidgeted with a lock of her lovely golden brown hair and began again. "After the operation I knew I had lost my attraction as a woman, but at least I had your friendship. I couldn't take your pity." She stared down at her feet.

"PITY!" Zak exploded. "You might have lost a breast, but the rest of you is still pretty amazing from where I'm sitting. I've been falling for you for weeks. You are still you even if there is a bit missing. Now, if you can get your head round that, can we start again?"

She grinned, nodding, and it was like the sun coming out. Suddenly the old easiness between them was *back and they chatted for ages. Then, remembering the paperwork still to do he said regretfully he would have to go. She stood up to see him out and Zak tentatively held out his arms. She stepped in, and he gave her a tender lingering kiss. To his surprise she returned the kiss and then some. He was definitely ready to stay longer and explore the possibilities but she pushed him to the door saying,*

"Enjoy the paperwork. Sweet dreams..."

Zak groaned and got into the car. Not sure what his driving was like but he arrived home without a single recollection of the journey and a silly smile on his face. The rest of the week went by in a blur and before he knew it, 5JR were finishing noting down the homework and waiting expectantly for the story.

oOo

As we neared Jerusalem I reflected that we had an easier time of it than expected. Perhaps just the sight of our troops had put off would be attackers. Ah, spoke too soon. I delivered my letters to the governor, who seemed pleased, unlike a couple of the court hangers on, Sanballat the Horonite and his sidekick, Tobiah the Ammonite. They seemed dismayed that we had come to help Jerusalem and I resolved to keep an eye on them.

For a few days I didn't do much more than ride round looking at the state of the place and chatting to people. I sneaked out in the night with a few trusted helpers and we saw for ourselves how bad the walls were. The massive gates were burned down and at least one of them was totally impassable. So, I called together the people, priests and officials and explained that God had laid on my heart to rebuild the city walls.

We got an enthusiastic reception until Sanballat, Tobiah and Geshem the Arab rushed up with their robes flapping, shouting that we were rebelling against the Babylonian king. I told them it was nothing to do with them and with angry murmurs from the crowd they slunk away. But, I had a feeling we had not heard the last from them. Great numbers of the city folk set to and began the rebuilding. Most worked just by their own houses, repairing the part nearest to them.

Zac had seen the puzzled look cross Isla's face and was not surprized when her hand waved in front of him. Resigned he said,

"Yes, Isla, what is it?"

"Sir, if all they were doing was their own patch of wall, why did they need Nehemiah to come from Babylon?"

"They didn't need him really, but sometimes it takes a bit of a push from a leader to get us going on something we know needs to be done."

Big Dave joined in,

"Like the playground litter picking, Sir?"

"Exactly. Now do you mind if I finish the story?"

A few of the nobles would not put themselves about to help build but most of the people helped in some way. There were enough workers to hew great beams of wood from the king's supplies and begin to rebuild the massive gates. Sanballat and his cronies mocked us with insults about how weak the wall was but we didn't let that put us off. Soon it was joined all the way round but was only half the height we needed. I think that was when our enemies began to be seriously alarmed and they plotted to raid us before the wall got higher.

We had the soldiers with us but that wasn't enough to protect the whole length so we hit on a plan. We split the workers into two groups. One lot carried on building while the others stood behind them holding weapons and coats of mail for themselves and the builders. They took turns at this. Those just carrying loads were encouraged to do that one handed and to hold a weapon in the other hand. We slept fully clothed with weapons close by. I even made one of the trumpeters stand near me so I could sound the alarm if an attack came.

Some of the hardships were from our own countrymen. Harvests had been poor and food was scarce. Some of the rich were grabbing houses and land or even enslaving people in return for food. I put a stop to it and made them give back what had been extorted. I was made governor of the province, but I wouldn't take the silver or the extra food that came with the job. In fact I still worked alongside the others on the wall and fed as many as I could with my own money. About one hundred and fifty people each day ate at my own tables and I paid for it all.

Sanballat, Tobiah and Geshem were very alarmed at our progress. When they realised how well prepared for battle we were, they abandoned plans for a direct attack. Instead the next ploy was to lure me away from the wall to meet them for a discussion. I refused and said I couldn't stop work for that. Another of their cronies suggested my life was in danger and wanted me to hide away in the Temple. I wasn't falling for such lies!

In spite of all the harassment we finished the whole length of the walls to the full height in only fifty-two days. It was a relief to know that the few poor souls still living in the city were now protected from raids. I was sure more would return when they heard it was safe. To make sure the people would live right and could ask for God's protection I got Ezra the priest to gather us all together and read God's law to us. When we all realised how badly we had let Him down over the years, many wept and felt ashamed. No wonder He had allowed Jerusalem to fall to an enemy army. But this was no time to weep now he was helping us to put things right. So I told them,

"The joy of the Lord is your strength,"

And I called for the old harvest feast to be celebrated, the feast of shelters. It was traditional to use branches to build little huts and to live in them for the seven days of the feast. So, we called on God to help us put right our way of life and looked to Him to guide and protect us in the future.

oOo

There was a ripple of applause as Zak finished the story. Some were chatting over what they had heard. Samira commented,

"He was very brave, Sir, and he must have really cared about people to make sure they all got fed."

"I think so, and he wanted them to change how they lived so that they would follow God and be safe."

Big Dave butted in,

"Sir, this will be our last lesson with you won't it.?"

"Yes, next Thursday will be the concert afternoon before we break up on Friday. There is a new RE teacher starting in September . In any case you will not all be in the same class next year."

Zak could see a couple of Isla's cronies digging her in the ribs and urging her to speak up so he nodded to her.

"We wondered if you could start a lunchtime story club , Sir, we would all like to hear some more."

His eyebrows lifted skywards but the clamour convinced him they were serious, so he promised to think about it and if he decided to do it he would send a note round at the beginning of the next term. With that Zak wished them good luck for their new classes and dismissed them. To his surprise there were thank you cards and little gifts dumped on the desk as they left. Quite a reversal from how the term began. Youngsters never ceased to amaze him.

CHAPTER SIX: BURNING AMBITION

It's not just pupils who delight in the freedom of the summer holidays: teachers are thrilled at the prospect of some time when they are not "on stage" or ploughing through endless piles of paper- work. Clothes can be scruffy, not smart, and the (possibly) glorious sunshine can be used for lazing around not playground duty.

Zak turned over, keeping his eyes tightly shut and resolutely ignoring the need to go to the bathroom. No, he was having a long lie in and NOTHING was going to stop him. Then his mobile gave out its vaguely eastern ring tone. Grr. Why did he think that one was less intrusive? Still keeping his eyes closed, he groped for the offending phone, tempted to throw it across the room. Instead he answered it. Angie's bright voice greeted him sounding surprised at his grumpy, "What?" the only word he had managed.

Undeterred she trilled on about what a beautiful day it was, suggesting a barbecue in the garden. He must have made the right noises as she hung up and left him in peace. He gave in and crawled out of bed and staggered to the bathroom. Feeling more human after a shower, he donned his oldest pair of ragged jeans and a very old Led Zeppelin tee shirt. Slumping down into a saggy armchair with a huge mug of coffee, he savoured the bliss of not having to work.

Soon he was letting himself into Angie's front door with a silly grin and a bag of soft drinks which he put in the fridge. At least he had the dress code right as she also had an old tee shirt on but in her case it was paired with a faded pair of skimpy shorts that certainly made the temperature rise! As he smooched over, she pushed a chopping board into his hands and left him to prepare the salad.

He managed to put up a fairly elderly and dusty gazebo to give them some protection from the blistering sun while Angie rummaged out some old vinyl records for the ancient gramophone he had bought at a car boot a few weeks ago. Then, loungers set up, drinks and salad fetched from the fridge, they were ready. Angie put on a record , saying,

"In honour of your tee shirt…"

Led Zeppelin played, "Going to California" as she served up red mullet coated in a zesty marinade and overlaid with the smoky tang of the barbecue. With salad piled up and loads of crusty soda bread they ate in silence, enjoying the moment. They took it in turns to pick out records, surprised that they both liked cheesy old rock or folk. Later, as they ate strawberries dipped in chocolate, they chatted about the theatre and books, finding more they had in common. Both of them enjoyed fantasy, from the serious and scary "Wheel of Time" saga by Robert Jordan, to Lindsay Buroker's more quirky and humorous offerings.

He told her to stay and rest while he cleared away and when he got back she was asleep. Smiling he adopted the pose of the Prince beside Sleeping Beauty and delicately kissed one eyelid. She woke and pulled his head down… He left the gazebo up for another day but cleared away the cooling barbecue and the record player *before he went home. The next day would not be so pleasant as he was to take her for a CT scan ready to begin radiotherapy. After arranging a pick- up time, he went home, planning a run once the day cooled down a bit.*

They were not at the hospital for long. Apparently it had been just to sort out the exact position of the treatment and to have a tattoo of little dots so they would get the same place every time. She was to go Monday to Friday at 9am for the next three weeks for the radiotherapy. He said he could take her except for two separate days when he had to be at school from early on for the students coming in for their exam results. She said she could get a taxi for those days, and not to worry.

It was not a pleasant few weeks for either of them. At first she wasn't affected much so they went on into town. She had been warned to stay out of the sun so they went round a shopping mall and had lunch out. She bought a few new cotton garments as she had been ordered not to wear man-made fabrics. After the first few treatments the side effects began to appear so he took her straight home each time, getting her some lunch ready and leaving it in the fridge until midday. He spent a lot of his time decorating his flat. If what he had planned for the future came off he might want to sell it so to get a good price it needed to look its best.

By the end of the holidays Angie's sessions had finished. But they had left her listless and tired, with blistered and darkened patches of skin. Even the hormone therapy which followed made her feel ill. Now came the hard slog through the exercises suggested by the physio and the climb back to fitness. Much of their spare time had been spent together lazing around indoors, watching films, reading or chatting.

However, all good things come to an end, and Zak had spent the final week of the summer break in school, putting up notices and signs to help the new entrants, working with the new staff and helping them become familiar with their roles. Each evening he went to Angie's to cook a meal for them both but left early, snowed under with paperwork. After two weeks they were all beginning to settle into the new routines allowing Zak to see if his extra

RE club were still up for lunch time sessions.. After much thought he had named it Hero Histories and put up a notice. Now, here he was on Thursday lunchtime waiting to see if anyone would turn up. It was no surprise to see Isla come in early, but it was quite a shock to see she had brough five from another group with her. That seemed to be the way of it, and he ended up with more than fifty students from right across the year group. He welcomed them, explained what the stories would be about, and began the first one of the new year.

oOo

Somehow I couldn't see myself as the sort who marches up to evil kings and challenges them, yet here I was. I was striding up to Ahab until I was practically nose to nose with him to give him a message he was not going to want to hear. The guards knew I was a prophet of God and let me get away with it. Anyone else would be wearing spears like a porcupine wears quills!

It was his own fault. He was without doubt the worst king we had ever had and was egged on in his wicked ways by his queen: Jezebel. Whatever had possessed him to choose her? She was a priestess of Baal, evil gods forbidden to our people. He was so besotted he built her a temple to one particular Baal, Melqart the Phoenician weather god. Goodness knows what went on in there but Oh, the rumours… Well, God had had enough and here was I sent to pronounce judgement on them and on the people for not stopping him. It was a brilliant judgement, asserting our God's authority over all nature, especially the weather.

"There will be no rain in the land except at God's word."

I turned and marched out leaving them all to make what they would of that. Perhaps they thought they could sit it out for a while and the rains would be sure to come back. The evil pair did not change their ways and famine stalked the land. At least God provided help for me. A little brook in the east of the country still held some water, and god sent me bread and meat via some ravens. It was boring fare but it kept me alive.

Unfortunately, even the brook dried up but God sent me to a place called Zarephath, again caring for me right in the middle of Melqart's own territory! He said someone could help me there. Not sure how that would work I made my way to the city and found a woman collecting some dry bits of wood outside the gate. We got talking. This poor widow and her young son had reached the end of their stores. The wood was for cooking one last bit of bread and after that they would starve to death. Nudged by God I asked her to prepare a little cake for me first and shrugging , she agreed so I went with her. Can you imagine what she thought when there was still as much flour and oil left even when she had fed me as well as herself and her son? In fact God promised that because she had been willing to give up some of her last bit of food for me, her flour and oil would not run out until the rains came again.

She had a spare room so I stayed and helped out where I could. Then, tragedy. Her young son took ill and died. In her distress she felt it was because she was not worthy to have me, a prophet staying with them. I took the body to my room and prayed asking God how he could allow this woman to suffer after she had helped me so much. He answered the prayer and the boy began to breathe. When he came round, healed, I took him back to his mother who said,

"Now I know that you truly are a prophet of God and all you say is true."

oOo

Just then the bell went and promising more next week they all dashed off to lessons. Zak was covering for Head of English while he met up with the Ofsted chap prior to an inspection later in the term.

That Saturday was another early start. Zak was qualified to drive the school minibus and it was his turn to take the football team and the PE staff to play in a nearby town. It was a chilly day for September but resisting the urge to slope off to a coffee bar, he stayed to cheer them on. It was a one all draw in the end but they were elated as the other team was rated the best in the schools' league and they had expected to lose. Back at school the three staff watched to see that everyone was picked up by family and then at last the rest of the weekend could begin.

After a hot lunch at Angie's Zak felt revived and asked what she wanted to do. She said she had read somewhere that the draining tiredness that the radiotherapy had caused could be alleviated by regular short walks. A watery sun was breaking through the clouds so he agreed and they set off. It was just a stroll around the block this first time so when her energy petered out they were not far from the house. Each day after he finished in school, they began to walk up the hill towards the town centre, going a little bit further every time.

When Thursday came around, Zak expected fewer to turn up to the club session. Instead there were some extra. All were attentive and well behaved but he decided to ask one or two RE staff if they would help the next time.

oOo

Three years of terrible hardship for the land had gone by before God sent me back into Israel to confront the king once more. On the way I met Obadiah, the highest official in the palace and one who had somehow managed to stay faithful to God. In fact, he had used his position to rescue about fifty of God's prophets. He hid them in a cave and got food to them, so Jezebel couldn't kill them. He was overjoyed to see me still alive. I said,

"What are you doing wandering the countryside alone?"

Apparently both he and Ahab were out searching for any grass still alive to give to the horses of the king's household as they were starving. I sent him off to find Ahab and bring him to me. As he was afraid I would vanish again I had to promise to stay in that spot. Finally, Ahab stormed up to me shouting,

"Ho you troubler of Israel."

Unimpressed, I reminded him that he was the one really troubling Israel by leading them astray to worship false gods. He looked ready to explode with rage so I said that he should bring all those false prophets of Melqart, about four hundred and fifty in all, to the top of Mount Carmel and to get all the people there to see what would happen next. He organised that.

There was a buzz of excitement from the vast crowd on the mountain top as I stepped forward to issue God's instructions.

"Why can't you make up your minds?" I shouted. "If Baal is really god, follow him But if The Lord is really God, follow Him. To help you, let's set up a little test. You prophets of Baal build an altar for a sacrifice to your god and I will build one for mine. Don't put a torch to the wood, we will just pray, and the god who answers with fire, he is god. The people roared their agreement while I gestured the others to go first. They built up the huge pile of wood fast enough, but then came the wait.

From morning until noon they leaped and cried and prayed, screaming for their puny god to send fire. When it got to midday I couldn't help taunting them, telling them to shout louder as he could be meditating or on a journey, or perhaps he was asleep. They cried louder and even cut themselves in a frenzy to try and make their god answer. At last about the time of the usual evening sacrifice they gave up in exhaustion and I got the people to come nearer to me.

First, I rebuilt the old broken down stone altar and heaped some wood on it, topping it off with the bull meat for the sacrifice. Then saying that was too easy, I got a few helpers to see if the mountain spring still had a drop of water. We poured twelve lots of water all over it until the wood was drenched and we even filled a trench around the altar. Then having made everything as difficult as possible, I prayed:

"Lord God of Abraham, Isaac and Israel, let it be known this day that you are God in Israel, and that I am your servant and have done all this because you told me to, and turn the hearts of the people back to you."

Fire fell, consuming not only the wood and the sacrifice, but was so intense that it licked up the water and crumbled the very stones to dust. The people fell on their faces to worship God. The false prophets were removed and rain came again that same evening, restoring the land.

oOo

Zak reached for his bottle of water to sooth his throat as a burst of applause rang out. One of the lads who had just come out of curiosity punched the air and shouted,

"That showed 'em, sir."

Everyone seemed full of enthusiasm so he agreed to carry on with the stories. They went off to class discussing what it would have been like to be in the crowd while Zak wondered how he could follow that.

CHAPTER SEVEN: TRANQUIL TIMES

Zak zoomed up the corridor like an Olympic power walker. Staff should not run except in dire emergencies. He had been waylaid by the head about something trivial (as usual) and now he was late for the storytelling club. As he turned the corner, he was amazed to see about fifty children lined up quietly outside the room they used. Isla was standing at the side looking authoritative while Big Dave loomed threateningly by her side. Not letting them see his amusement he waved them inside, stuck a bottle of water on the desk and waited for them to settle so he could begin the next story.

My father, David the Giant Killer, was a hard act to follow. After he became King he had cut our neighbouring kingdoms (who all wanted our land) down to size. It was beginning to look as if all I would need to do as the next king would be to sit on a fancy throne and look pretty! When he could see there was no one left to fight, my Father consulted God about building a proper Temple instead of the tent one we had carried with us since the desert times after Egypt. Surprisingly, he was refused permission. God said it was not a job for a man of war and he was saving the task for me. Mind you, although father was obedient he was also determined. If he wasn't allowed to build it, fine, but he set about collecting necessary materials. You have never seen such quantities of silver and gold for the vessels and to ornament the place, as well as vast stores of more mundane materials. He never did things by halves. He even had the plans drawn up ready. He really was an unstoppable force when he had ideas about something.

You can imagine how I felt when I eventually became king. God must have realised how unsure of myself I was, as He met with me in a dream. He asked what I would like Him to give me. It didn't require too much thought because there was a problem weighing heavily on my mind. From now on, the thousands of people in the country would look to me for help. I would have to make countless decisions that would affect their lives. So I asked for the wisdom needed to govern them well.

God was delighted that this was my request instead of wanting riches or a long life. In fact, He promised to give me not just the wisdom I needed but riches and honour as well. Even my life would be long if I followed Him and obeyed Him.

When I woke up, the whole dream stayed with me so vividly that I realised the conversation had been real. I felt so much gratitude that I gave a thanksgiving offering to God and ordered a feast for all the servants in the palace. There was not long before that special wisdom was needed.

One of the ways I was going to use all the extra wisdom God promised me was to offer a way for ordinary people to get justice if they felt the usual system did not serve them. So, I held courts where they could come before me and plead their cause. It was often a challenge to find satisfactory answers. Such a case concerned two women who were brought into court, one with a baby in her arms. They were dressed in the kind of flashy clothes which suggested their profession. They lived in the same household and had both given birth within days of each other.

One baby had died, and there seemed to be a dispute as to who owned the living child. There were no witnesses so it was going to be up to me to determine who was telling the truth. I thought hard until what I knew of motherhood suggested a trick I might try. I took one of the guards aside and warned him to look stern and go along with what I asked, assuring him it would be all right. I called the women forward to me for the judgement. In a loud voice I commanded the soldier to take his sword and cut the baby in half, giving each woman half the child.

Horrified gasps and murmurs went around the court. As I watched closely one woman just shrugged in agreement but the other one, distraught, fell to her knees before me and cried,

"Oh great King, give the baby to her to bring up, but keep it alive."

Obviously the first knew the baby wasn't hers and didn't care what happened to it. I bade the guard give the child to the woman who wished to save its life. Relieved smiles from the courtiers greeted the judgement and that case furthered my reputation for wisdom and fairness.

oOo

The shrill call of the bell for afternoon classes had them all scrambling to their feet, Zak promised to try to be on time for their next session when he would continue the story. Many of the students thanked him as they rushed off.

On the following Wednesday evening Zak drew the car up outside Angie's and just sat for a moment, almost too weary to get out. The mini Ofsted was over and had gone well for the most part. It was never pleasant being watched constantly under the critical eye of someone assessing your every word and mannerism. He had to admit that the older lady assigned to him appeared to know what she was talking about and she had an easy manner and a twinkle in her eye.

Unfortunately the one assigned to the science department was cold and clinical and seemed unaware of the finer points of teaching a potentially hazardous subject. Young Patrick, in his first few weeks of teaching, had walked out after half a day of the Ofsted experience. Zak had been sent by the Head to try and talk him out of his resignation. Instead, aware of the discipline problems he had and his growing dislike of the classroom, Zak had gone armed with career information. They discussed other uses of his qualifications and the lad seemed more settled and hopeful. You needed to be a born actor and a bit larger than life to survive in front of thirty students.

The supply teacher who had taken over at very short notice was just such a character. She obviously loved the job and they responded to her. She would stay until they found someone. She was looking for a permanent post having just moved to the area with her partner, and Zak hoped she would apply. Shaking himself out of the stupor he was in, he climbed out of the car and went into the cottage. Angie had seen him arrive and poured him a beer, not making any attempt to talk, she dished up the homemade quiche and pushed across the bowl of salad so he could help himself. Unusually she had also made a dessert, sticky toffee pudding, and after a second helping he began to feel human again. She really was a good cook and had taken over weekdays while he cooked for them at the weekends.

They chatted happily about their day. She had begun writing and had really enjoyed the background research into the period of history in which her novel would be set. It was lovely to see her beginning to feel stronger and getting some enjoyment from life again.

During assembly the next day, the head thanked the students for the way they had coped with the few days of Ofsted. She praised the staff for their calm professionalism. Zak smothered a smile as he noticed a few shared grimaces among the younger staff who had found it so hard.

At lunchtime he made a special effort to be early for the story club and they looked pleasantly surprised to see him already in the room when they arrived. Wasting no

*time, he began and the stragglers had to creep in and sit
at the back.*

oOo

During those early years of my reign we began
work on the Temple. Since I had continued my Father's
friendly relationship with Hiram king of Tyre I paid him to
supply the great cedar trees which grew in his country.
Between us we hit on the idea of strapping them together
in great rafts and floating them south along the coasts to
my country. That left a much shorter journey overland to
Jerusalem.

As every inner wall was to be lined with the fragrant
wood, you can imagine how much was needed. We sent
workmen there to help, 10,000 a month in shifts. They
spent one month there and then two months at home.
Much of it was carved with the shapes of gourds and
flowers. In the inner sanctuary, wood was not special
enough so we overlaid it with pure gold. Chains of gold
separated this area off from the rest. 70,000 worked on
the actual construction.

Hiram also sent skilled metalworkers to oversee the bronze casting of the vessels we would use, including a huge one called a Sea of Bronze to meet the need we would have for water in the Temple. Two massive bronze pillars marked the outer doorway.

Luckily, we had no shortage of fine stone and there were some excellent stonemasons to carve it. With such a holy site we thought it best to preserve its peaceful atmosphere so all the dressing of the stone was done at the quarry itself. Then the stone was brought to the Temple ready to be placed in position. 80,000 stonecutters worked on the task. In the eleventh year of my reign, seven years after we had begun, the work was completed. I was able to get the priests to place into the holy inner area the ark containing Moses' stone tablets where God had written ten commands for us to keep. Soon we had transferred all the immense quantities of gold and silver vessels my father had prepared for the new Temple. It took a while and it seemed good to time the dedication of such an important place to coincide with our new year. So about eight months passed. Now, all was ready for a grand opening ceremony. After the people gathered together in front of the Temple, Priests carried in the Ark of the Covenant. Inside it were the two blocks of stone Moses brought down the mountain for us. God had written the ten commands on them to show us how His people should live. As soon as the Ark was brought in, clouds of glory filled the place. I was awestruck. It was just like the Presence of God in the cloud leading us through the desert in the stories of our flight from Egypt.

We got through the speech everyone was expecting, then we came to the important part, a prayer of dedication. I had thought about this a lot. The whole point of the Temple was for there to be a place people could always feel they could meet with our God. So, I simply asked if He would listen to them when they called on Him at the Temple when there was trouble in the land. I mentioned the ways we might let Him down and asked if He would listen and help us if we asked for forgiveness. This all took a while, and so did the sacrifices. But then we had prepared an eight day feast for the whole country as many could not make the journey to Jerusalem.

After that God appeared to me a second time, to reassure me:

"If my people who are called by My Name, humble themselves, pray and seek My face and turn from their wicked ways then I will hear from Heaven and will forgive their sin and heal their land."

However, He did warn me that if they were not faithful to Him they would be cast out of the land and the Temple would be torn down. That seemed a fair bargain to me.

My Father, David had prepared such vast quantities of materials that I was minded to continue building, and for another thirteen years we kept going. A Hall of the Throne came next where the people could come for justice, and then a splendid palace. Tributes came in from the rulers of many kingdoms and there was so much gold that the plates and drinking vessels in the palace were all made of it. Silver was counted too common! God had more than fulfilled all His promises to me.

People came from other lands to consult me when they had hard problems to solve. However, one turned up with ulterior motives. She did not really believe my reputation and came to test me with hard questions. To put herself on an equal footing she brought a vast retinue, and camels loaded with spices and gold as gifts for me. But, when we had talked and she had seen the riches of the palace and the way we governed, the Queen of Sheba had to admit that not only were all the tales true, but she had not been told even the half of the real splendour. She went away much chastened.

oOo

Isla said as I finished,

"Sir was he a good king right until he died?

"No, he turned away from God and on his death the kingdom was split up because of it. But some of his wisdom has lasted even until now and we can read about it in the Book of Proverbs in the Bible. Interestingly, as an old man he offered one piece of useful advice,

'Remember your Creator in the days of your youth before the difficult days come and the years draw near when you will say I have no pleasure in them.' "

"Aw sir, that's a bit grim," butted in big Dave.

"Yes, let's just remember his early days as the wisest ruler any nation ever had. See you next week. Sam, you left your glasses case, it's on the floor." She turned back to fetch it as they rushed off to lessons, chatting about Solomon as they went.

CHAPTER EIGHT: FRIEND OR FOE?

As I sat down in my office after year five's history, there was a tentative knock at the door. Not the Head who would just have barged in. Not a friend as they would have peered round the door to see how welcoming I looked. Child?

"Yes," I said in a forbidding voice hoping they would take the hint and go away. No such luck. Ben from my story group sidled in and said,

" 'Ave you gorra minute ,sir?

Sighing, I pushed away the history tests I was about to mark and prepared to listen. He explained that he and his friends were worried about Big Dave. Because of his size and being handy with his fists a gang of much older boys had accepted him and he was trailing round the streets with them at night.

He wouldn't listen to Isla who had tried to talk him out of it. Isla had met his Mum who knew what was happening but also said she couldn't get through to him.

That did make me worry because he was usually close to his Mum and had helped her a lot since his Dad died a few years earlier. I said,

"Leave it with me; I'll try to think of something."

"I knewed you would ,sir."

And with that final mangling of the Queen's English he left me to my marking.

Later, as I scoffed my share of Angie's delicious cottage pie and home-grown cabbage I told her all about Big Dave.

"Isn't he in your story club? Why not use one of your hero tales to make him think?"

I refused a third helping, knowing I would have to run much further to work off what I had already eaten. An idea hit me. A perfect story for this situation…

For once, I was on time for the story club and we all settled in to explore the foibles of our next character. I explained that this one was further back in time from Solomon. In fact he came later in the group of judges after

Gideon we had heard of , long before there were any kings in Israel. They had relapsed into bad ways again and for forty years God had been allowing the mighty Philistine army to harass the land hoping they would turn back to him and ask for help

oOo

It is a great nuisance, not being able to cut your hair. I tied it up into a tight knot each morning but as I worked it slipped loose and had to be re-done. Yes, it was definitely a nuisance. So, why didn't I cut it then? Well, it was all to do with my strange birth. My parents couldn't have children but my mother prayed so desperately to God for a family that he took pity on her and here I am! Part of that prayer was that I would be set apart for God to use for his purposes and as a sign of that, I was not to drink anything alcoholic and my hair would never be cut.

I ask you, is it fair to drop all that on a fella without even asking. Still, it has its good side. I seem to be very strong for my size and the ladies do seem to like that and the long hair also seems to appeal…

Now the story begins when I had got to know one of the Philistine girls living in a nearby occupied area. Yes, all right, she was one of the enemy but I had fallen for her in a big way. It was while I was walking to visit her that I got attacked by a lion. Don't panic! I was so strong that even without a weapon I was able to subdue it and then kill it. I left the carcass a little way off the road and carried on my journey. There were many trips back and forth along the road to visit her and when I went to look what had happened to the lion's body, a swarm of bees had made a home in the picked clean skeleton. It amused me and I grabbed a bit of the honeycomb to eat as I walked along.

Eventually I managed to persuade my parents to negotiate a marriage with this girl, much against their better judgement. The great day arrived. They had prepared for the usual days of feasting and we joined with her family and Philistine friends, thirty of them in all. It made for a slightly uneasy atmosphere all round. The usual entertainment of music and stories and puzzles went on and I finally set a riddle I was sure they couldn't solve. I was so sure in fact that we had a wager going. I bet them thirty sets of clothes for them all that they would not get it before the end of the feasting. What was it? I made it up from my experience with the lion:

"Out of the eater came something to eat

Out of the strong came something sweet."

It was quite amusing to hear the pathetic guesses but I didn't realise how greedy they were or how much they would influence my new wife. She pouted that I didn't love her enough to tell her and wheedled the answer out of me.

Of course the next day their ringleader sidled up and said with a smirk,

"What is stronger than a lion and what is sweeter than honey?"

Realising I had been duped, I put aside my new wife and stormed off. I wanted nothing to do with them ever again. I think they married her off to someone else. The bet? Oh yes, I paid up but at their expense. In fact I single-handedly killed thirty of the Philistines and dumped their garments with the ones who had cheated me. Their raids intensified but I was able to defeat them every time.

Unfortunately they remembered my weakness for a pretty face and when I sneaked into their capital city to see the ravishingly beautiful Delilah I was captured. The laugh was on them, though, as I broke down their city gates to escape. With my great strength I carried them away with me! Cunningly they plotted with Delilah to find out the secret of my strength so that they would be able rid themselves of me.

I couldn't help myself. Back I went, enjoying the flattery as she admired my power and physique. When she asked the secret I lied to her and told her if I was bound with new bowstrings they would weaken all that strength. On my next visit, they had supplied her with the strings and she bound me as I slept. When the Philistine soldiers broke in I burst the strings and killed them all.

In my pride, I thought I could always escape so I went back to her. I lied to her that new ropes would cancel out my strength. They also allowed me to escape and wreak vengeance on another lot of soldiers. Then I told Delilah if my hair was woven into the threads of the heavy wooden loom in her room I would not be able to escape but of course I did.

Time and again when I visited she begged to know my secret. Like a stupid fool I finally gave in and explained my strength came from our God and that to signify being set apart to Him I was never to cut my hair. That night as I slept she cut all my hair off and when her friends rushed in they were able to defeat me at last and carry me off.

oOo

Zak had finished early but when everyone demanded to know what happened to Samson he gave the rather grisly end to the tale. The Philistines had blinded him and set him to work with the oxen, turning a huge millstone to grind corn. He had nothing else to think about but how he had let God down by his choice of wrong friends. After a long while his hair had begun to grow back and almost unnoticed his strength began to return. The end of his story came when a great feast was held for the

Philistine Lords in the Temple of their god Dagon. When they were thoroughly drunk they demanded that Samson should be brought out so they could taunt and make fun of him. Servants led him in and allowed him to prop himself up against two of the immense stone pillars supporting the roof. With a mighty heave he pushed them apart and the roof fell in. Not only did it crush their false idol Dagon, and the Philistine Lords, but also Samson himself perished. But with his death the land was at peace and the raids ended.

It was a subdued group that made their way out leaving behind Big Dave to talk to Zak. He poured out what had been happening to him with the gangs and asked what he should do. Zak said that when you have been given great strength like Samson, it is to protect the weak and care for them. He advised Dave to stay in at night for a while and then to stick with those of his own age.

As he headed for his office, Ben sidled up to him saying,

"That wore smashing, Sir. I reckon it did the trick all right. Tara."

Over tea he told Angie who said she had known he would think of something. Laughing, he replied that was kind of what Ben had said and repeated his strange version of their Mother tongue.

CHAPTER NINE: HOPE

At last it was Christmas Day. The past few weeks had been fraught at work. 'Flu had nearly seen off the Christmas concert, but the stand-ins had done really well. Zak had done a lot more actual teaching than usual to free up the necessary staff for rehearsals and still had to fit in his usual admin chores. Ah well, he could now relax and try to digest the huge dinner Angie and he had prepared together.

With his long legs spread out on the sofa and his head in her lap he beamed up at her. She giggled, asking him what the self- satisfied look was all about.

"Just thinking we should open the pressies. If we wait any longer it will be Boxing day."

Soon bags and wrapping paper were strewn across the floor. Both of their families had sent gifts which they had saved to open together. His elderly Aunt had sent lurid purple socks with a matching tie so Angie made him put them on. Weak with laughter it was a while before they could get any further. One of Angie's distant cousins topped that, though, with an obviously handmade and out of shape orange cardie. Zak said to keep it for the power cuts later in the winter and they started laughing again.

Their gifts to each other were more of a success and were along the same lines though they had kept them secret. She had bought him a new leather brief case having noticed his old one was steadily falling apart. His for her was a wonderfully soft leather handbag in exactly the shade of grey of her new shoes. She squealed with delight as she had been trying unsuccessfully to find one since she bought the shoes. Of course, that deserved a kiss!

Some time later they swished the empty wrappings around to see if anything else lurked underneath. Zak fished in his pocket and said,

"There's just one more."

Dropping to his knees in front of where she sat, he said,

"These last few months have been very precious to me, and I want us to be so much more than friends or partners. Marry me."

Opening the little box, he passed her the antique, rose-gold and diamond, boat shaped ring he had found in the local antique centre way back in October.

Instead of putting it on, she looked up at him with a serious face and unshed tears in her lovely grey eyes.

"What if the cancer comes back? You don't want saddling with a liability.

"Oh, my love, we will face the future together. I would sooner have a short time with you than fifty years with anyone else."

In an attempt to lighten the mood, he waggled his eyebrows suggestively and added, "After all, if I am going to look after you anyway, I may as well be entitled to all the fringe benefits!" It worked. She laughed and flung a cushion at him before putting on the ring. It was a bit loose, so Zak suggested that they take it to a jeweller to get it altered and buy wedding rings at the same time. He could tell she loved it as much as he had hoped she would. When the passionate kisses that followed began to get out of hand, they decided to clear up all the wrapping paper and wash up. As Christians they both felt it was wrong to anticipate their marriage.

On Boxing Day Zak drove them both a short way out of town to a small lake and they began to walk and plan for a wedding on Easter Saturday with a short honeymoon in the first of Zak's two weeks holiday to follow. Angie had brought turkey sandwiches, some Christmas cake and a flask of tea, so they sat for a while on an old, felled tree trunk and had lunch. With so many things to discuss, before they knew it, they were right round the water and back to their starting point. A brilliant, deep red sunset streaked with bars of grey cloud sent them back to the car thinking of hot coffee and mince pies as the cold intensified.

Angie had news to share. She had an email from the publisher who had been considering the first few chapters of her book. They liked it and were going to pay her an advance and had set her a reasonable date later in the year for her to submit the finished work. So, she would not be going back to teaching at all. They discussed other opportunities such as articles for magazines, or paid talks.

All too soon the new term began. In the few days after New Year Zak had put his flat on the market. It seemed unlikely to sell in the depths of winter but he wanted to sort things out as soon as possible. It was hard to focus on school but he tried to nail the story of another hero for his group. The one he chose was a character who lived in tempestuous times. On the Thursday lunchtime he watched his eager group assemble and smiled to himself thinking that these were the folk who hated RE. As soon as they settled in, he began.

The bruised man in the dirty brown robe looked up at the concerned faces around him. He was overwhelmed by the emotion of what had befallen his master and friend and begged for a few moments to collect his thoughts so that he could tell the story properly. Someone thrust a small stoneware goblet of cheap wine into his hand and he sipped it gratefully. Then he began his harrowing tale.

"Most of you know me as Baruch the scribe, and I used to help a lot of you with letters and official documents but over the last few years I have mostly helped Jeremiah. He needed someone to write copies of the prophecies which God constantly gave him to tell His people. But I get ahead of myself. You need to know a bit about Jeremiah. He was born into a priestly family, so I suppose from a young age he expected to serve God in some way. But I don't think he saw himself becoming God's mouthpiece giving some very unpalatable words to His wayward and wicked people. After all, everyone knew that prophets were grey bearded ancient dodderers, and he was only about twenty-three years old at the time.

Of course, he protested that he couldn't speak well and wasn't much more than a child, but God always chooses the person with the right attitude and equips him along the way. Mind you, at least He promised to make Jeremiah a 'fortified wall of bronze' meaning, I suppose, that no one would be able to stop him. He was quite shy and sensitive so the role he had to play must have been torture for him. Still, perhaps that made it obvious that the words were all God's because he was not the kind of person to pretend to be important.

Basically, his message was that God had seen His people's wicked ways and if they didn't change, He was going to allow their enemies to overrun them. Young King Josiah and his wise advisor took over the country. They found a big, neglected book of God's laws and began to call the land to better ways. It was working, but then after twelve years Josiah was killed and none of the rulers after Him were any good at all. They led the people further astray.

Jeremiah spoke out fearlessly. Unfortunately, they wouldn't listen. God even used to suggest little parables to make the message clearer. I remember one good one. Jeremiah was sent to the potter's workshop just to watch what he was doing. On the wheel was a large vase which was just having the last bit of shaping completed. The potter's hand slipped a little and the shape was spoilt. With a sigh the potter smashed down the clay, cut it from the wheel, wedged it to get the air out and began again. God told Jeremiah that His people were marred like the vase and they would be smashed down and rebuilt. Not that they took any notice, if anything things got worse. Some of the depraved people were even killing children for the evil foreign gods.

Jeremiah was hated for speaking out against all this. Even the priests who should be living holy lives and receiving the same messages from God were just as evil. One of them, named Pashur, had Jeremiah beaten and put in the stocks. He came to a bad end because of it. Believe it or not, one of the kings, Zedekiah, even had the nerve to ask Jeremiah to plead to God for help when Nebuchadnezzar king of Babylon was on his way to attack them. How do you think God liked that? He sent the reply that not only would He not save the land, but He would also fight against them. Their only hope was to surrender and go with the Babylonians to their land. Any who disobeyed and stayed would die by the sword and disease.

Our prophet was reviled as a traitor while false prophets assured everyone that things would be all right. Jeremiah continued to speak out, telling any who would listen that God had prepared a hope and a future for them if they would mend their ways, and would help those taken away to believe and serve Him again. Eventually, God would restore them to their own land. In the end, they decided to shut Jeremiah up permanently and threw him into an old water cistern that had dried to just mud. He sank in and they left him for dead.

A foreigner in the king's household, an Ethiopian, had more belief and feeling than God's people. He pleaded to be allowed to save Jeremiah's life and they finally agreed. He was hauled out. Shortly afterwards the land was conquered by Nebuchadnezzar and the Babylonian army. Many were killed, but because the Ethiopian had trusted God, he was kept safe. The young and those who believed Jeremiah were taken to Babylon. Meanwhile the poor and the old were left to work the land as best they could. Jeremiah and I stayed to help them.

Even so rebellion was still in their hearts, and they murdered the governor left by Nebuchadnezzar to oversee us. Despite Jeremiah warning everyone not to go they decided to drag us all to Egypt thinking we would be safe, but I knew God's terrible judgement would follow us even there. The worst of it is I have no idea what has happened to my old friend, he is missing. As my anguish got the better of me, I stopped speaking, choked by my tears. A couple of those with me glanced at each other and said there was a rumour he had been stoned to death. In the days that followed we searched and questioned those who had come to Egypt with us, but we were not able to find out what had happened to Jeremiah, God's faithful prophet. What he left behind was a legacy of hope for God's people if they would only believe and obey."

For a moment the group were all quiet until Ben broke in,

"Whew, that wor grim, Sir."

"Yes, I'm afraid heroes are not always appreciated. Despite their best efforts, they sometimes fail. During the worst time Jeremiah always offered hope to anyone who would listen."

Isla, always thoughtful, said,

"He was fantastically brave, sir. Do you think he ever wondered if he had got it all wrong?"

"Mmm…perhaps. But don't forget, what he said came true, so it proved that his words were from God. Interestingly, the Babylonians themselves had a prophecy against them for attacking God's people even though they deserved it. The city would be destroyed and never rebuilt. It is still only a ruin to this day."

That got a "Wow" from the group. The end of lunch bell cut short any more discussion and they all hurried off.

Never had the weeks sped by so fast. The flat sold. Much of the furniture was taken on by the young couple who were buying it as their first home but some of his personal things needed packing and moving. He moved into lodgings for the last few weeks. Somehow, he also managed to fit in a weekend course on management for people considering headships and a couple of job interviews. Both were good schools. One, it was obvious that all the interviewers had someone in mind. He was offered the other one but after spending the day in the school he felt it was a well- oiled machine and he would not be able to bring much to it, so he turned it down.

That left one more interview in the last few days of term. His head was being really understanding and was prepared to let him go straight after Easter if he got the job as she knew they had been without a head for some time. Knowing he was pushing his luck, he knocked on her door on Friday afternoon when nearly everyone else had gone home. Her smile indicated a fairly good mood, so he took a deep breath and said,

"You remember I have Wednesday off for that interview?

"Yers…" the smile faded a bit.

"Could I have Tuesday as well? Angie has a scan and an interview with her cancer specialist, and I don't want her to face it alone. It would mean a lot to us. She hasn't got a nearby relative to help."

The head agreed, and after chatting a bit about the wedding plans, he went back to his own office to finish off some marking before heading for Angie's.

On the Tuesday morning he was awake early. His nerves wouldn't let him nod off again, so he was early at Angie's. Apparently, she had the same problem as she was sitting in her armchair with her jacket on, ready to go. Consequently, they had a long time to sit in the waiting room before she was called in for the scan. There was another long wait for the blood test but after her number flashed up on the screen, she was in for only a few moments. They had lunch in the hospital restaurant. Zak supposed it was quite nice but by now he was so worked up it tasted like cardboard. Angie must have felt the same as she pushed her plate aside with the food only half eaten. He murmured,

"This is ridiculous, let's have a quiet prayer."

In that otherwise empty corner of the dining room, they held hands and shared how they felt with God saying they accepted whatever He had in store for them

There was yet another long wait before they were ushered into the consulting room. He shook hands with them both and with the usual caveats of, "it's early days yet," and, "we can't be sure," he finally told them that Angie seemed to be clear of the cancer. They laughed and cried at the same time and clung to each other, sharing with the specialist that it was only a week to their wedding which they could now approach in an easier frame of mind. He warned them that there would be annual check-ups until five years after the operation, but it was now looking promising. With lighter hearts they made their way back to the car, appreciating the early daffodils in the flower beds and the warm, spring sunshine.

CHAPTER TEN: CHALLENGE AND CHANGE

During his hasty breakfast a text came in on his mobile. Just a couple of words from Angie,

"Good luck!"

He smiled and grabbing the briefcase she gave him for Christmas, he went out to the car. The school wasn't far away so he arrived much too early as usual. After he parked, it was such a nice morning he sat on the low wall of the car park watching the youngsters arrive. One came by exhibiting such skill dribbling a football he shouted '

Are you in the school team?

The lad's face fell, and his mate shouted back,

"We daren't play him. He's like lightening but he can't remember which end to run to and he scores for the other side."

The lads ran off and still chuckling to himself, Zak made his way into the slightly crumbling front entrance.

A slightly older man was seated on one of the shabby blue armchairs while a beautifully coiffured lady in an elegant emerald green suit was chatting to a lady with a clipboard. After directing the other interviewee to a seat, the clipboard lady came over and introduced herself as Karen, the deputy head. She took Zak's name and got him seated saying they were just waiting for Mr Hancock. At that point a young man who could have passed as a Hollywood A-lister strolled in and gave Karen the benefit of his 100 -watt smile. She was apparently immune and after ticking his name on the list she explained how the day would work.

Before coffee, they would familiarise themselves with the place, then after, they were each to give their short presentation to the governors and County officials. Following lunch, individual interviews would close the day and they hoped to appoint someone by the end of the process. Pointing out the cloakrooms to the right of the main office she began their tour of the school. Karen and her clipboard led a brisk march along the rather dingy corridors. Most classrooms they just peeped through the glass doors or observed through the corridor windows. Zak was less than impressed to see the fed-up looks of the children mirrored on the faces of equally depressed teachers. It seemed to be putting off the other candidates but, strangely, it made Zak want the job more. He KNEW he could fire enthusiasm and make the place somewhere everyone wanted to be.

They did go into one classroom, obviously handpicked. In it a young teacher, not long out of college, was encouraging small groups to discuss ideas about how emerging countries could develop their economies without damaging the environment. The children were all engaged and enthusiastic. As they left, Zak hung back for a moment to whisper to the teacher about how impressed he was, then hurried off to catch the others.

After coffee and a short comfort break, they were called in one at a time to give their presentations to four of the school governors and three of the education department at County Hall. Zak did not have to wait too long as he was second. He was shown to the laptop and projector and hoping for no technical hitches he put in his

USB stick with his headings and illustrations. Sighing with relief that everything worked he went through his presentation covering all he hoped to do in the school to make a difference. He described the importance of good relationships with the parents and the community and lifting the morale of the teachers by boosting their professional skills. He described how he wanted to heighten the aspirations of the children in what was essentially a traditional working class catchment area. He came to a finish almost to the last second of his allotted time and thanked them for listening. He collected his memory stick and took a seat back in the waiting area.

To pass the time he texted Angie about how it was going so far, then scribbled a few notes of extra things he wanted to mention in the interview if he was given an opening. Soon they were all shown into a side room where tables were set for lunch. It was a bit of an ordeal, but he did manage to chat to the governors who were seated on either side of him. They were given a few minutes to freshen up and Zak seized the chance to stroll into the spring sunshine and get some fresh air.

Back in the dingy entrance area Zak had to wait far longer this time as the order had been changed and he was to be the last one in. He amused himself by thinking of the shades of paint he would use to brighten the place up and what kind of comfortable seating might be found. At last, he was called in and was given a seat facing his seven inquisitors. Mostly they questioned some of the points from his presentation which gave him a chance to pour out what he felt he could do with the school. By now, it had begun to feel like adopting an unwanted orphan and the depth of feeling for this run- down school surprised even him.

As 5pm approached they gathered up papers, whispered to one another and all nodded. The chair of governors said,

"We would be pleased to offer you the post. I understand you are able to take it up after Easter. Do you wish to accept?

With a delighted grin Zak said, "Oh yes," and they all shook hands with him. Karen showed him out of a second door which led to the office so that they could discuss arrangements while the news was broken to the other candidates. He told Karen that he would expect to meet with staff for two days during the second week of the holiday and found that she had already planned that. He knew she would be a very good second in command and he suspected he would need all the help he could get.

With the feeling that perhaps the celebratory dinner with Angie might have gone on too long the night before, Zak set off extra early on Thursday for what would be his last day at school. By 7.30am he had pressganged the caretaker into helping him clear out his office and load the car so that it would be easier after school. By 8.15am he was finishing off notes for the new timetable and writing up some of the tasks the acting deputy would have to cover in the summer term.

Finally, the thing he had dreaded was upon him. The final session with his story telling club. They filed in looking very subdued having been told of his promotion in Assembly that morning. Isla said with tears in her eyes,

"We'll miss you, Sir."

Elbowing her in the ribs for being soppy, Big Dave broke in with,

"Ave you gorra good story for the last one, Sir?"

"You bet," said Zak, cheerfully, "listen to this…"

oOo

I was only a youngster when Nebuchadnezzar invaded but it was obvious even to me that God would not help us as people did not really have faith anymore. My three best friends and I tried to stay together when all of the young people were marched away to Babylon. At first it was hard to keep up, but we were on the road for five months so by the end we were fit and could go as fast as the soldiers.

We expected to be turned into slaves or to have to work in the fields, but no, the king realised we were bright and he had plans for us. We were to live in the palace and be taught the language and lots of important subjects. We were all given Babylonian names too. I didn't like the name Belteshazzar and would rather have stayed as Daniel but you can't argue with the king. We were given the same rich food as the King's table but the four of us pleaded to be given vegetables and water instead of the food and wine. You see, we had worked out that it was offered up to the false gods before being served. The four of us were determined to stay faithful to our God, no matter what happened.

The man in charge was afraid he would be punished if we looked sickly and there were questions asked, so he refused. I suggested trying it out for a month and if we looked ill we would give in. He agreed and when they checked up on us, we were healthier than all those who had eaten the king's food.

(Samia, the vegetarian in the story club punched the air and shouted, "YES!" but she was shushed by the rest.)

God gave us skill and great learning so that by the time we were tested we were very much more knowledgeable than all the rest of the exiled youngsters. Jobs were found among the government advisors for all four of us. Mind you, I very nearly lost my life not long afterwards. The King was in a great panic one morning having woken from a very disturbing dream. He felt it might foretell the future, so he sent for the advisors to explain it to him. Obviously they had misled him before, for when they made soothing noises and told him to recount the dream, he refused. He demanded that they gave the dream as well as its interpretation. That was preposterous as only the gods could do that, but he insisted and sentenced them to death. I worked for the same department and was being dragged out with them to be executed but I had an idea. I persuaded them to wait a few days. In the meantime, my three friends and I prayed. God answered and showed me the dream and what it meant so I asked to be taken to the King.

I told him he had dreamed of a great statue made of many different materials from a gold head to feet of clay. A boulder had struck the feet and grown into a great mountain. I explained each material was representing a different kingdom in the future after his golden age. The mountain was a kingdom which would never be destroyed.

He was astonished and admitted that our Jewish God was the God of gods. He made me ruler of all Babylon and I was able to appoint my three friends to share the kingdom under me. We made a great team, and we were appreciated by the next three kings also.

Many were jealous of our success and tried to destroy us. God helped us to survive -sometimes in very dramatic ways. Now, I am over eighty years old and the deadliest of all plots was hatched against me only a short while ago. My fellow satraps (governors) in their jealousy were determined to remove me but I tried to live in such a way that they could not accuse me of any wrongdoing. In their frustration they came up with a fool proof plan. They wormed their way into the king's good books with lots of lavish flattery. When he was well and truly hooked, they suggested a new law for the space of thirty days, that no one should pray to any gods for anything but only petition him. Anyone who disobeyed was to be thrown to the lions in the palace menagerie. King Darius thought this was a delightful idea and readily signed it leaving the plotters chortling with glee.

I heard the proclamation, of course. Was I about to change my ways for a month? Not even for a day would I stop praying to my God who had saved my life so many times and blessed me so richly. As usual, three times a day I put down my mat by the open window which faced Jerusalem our beloved home and I lifted up my hands to bless the Lord's name and pray to him. My enemies were waiting nearby so they and their witnesses rushed off to tell the king. I was arrested and dragged into the court.

Darius was devastated. He and I were great friends and worked together for the good of the kingdom. The law once signed could not be changed but he laboured until sunset to try to find a way out. Finally, he had to admit it was hopeless and he accompanied me when soldiers brought me to the pit where the lions were. As they lowered me down into it, he said,

"May your God whom you serve deliver you…" and he sealed the stone at the entrance with his signet ring.

Apparently, he would not eat and stayed up all night. He forbade them to bring any of his wives to him to distract him and paced the floor until the very first rays of light crept over the horizon. Then he hastened out to the menagerie and shouted down,

"Has the God you serve been able to deliver you?"

I was able to shout back, joyously,

"Oh King, live forever! God sent His angel to shut the lions' mouths and they have not harmed me."

When the soldiers had lifted me out, Darius commanded that those who accused me were to be thrown to the lions in my place. With fearful shrieks, they tippled down into the pit and were set upon by the lions straight away. Darius wrote a proclamation to his empire that the God of the Jews is the Living God who delivers and rescues, working signs and wonders in heaven and on earth. So, praise be, I lived to tell my story.

Zac finished this last story with a solemn word to remember to have faith and to serve God so that He would lead and protect them always. Then they all clapped and cheered while Isla dragged a parcel out of her bag and brought it out to him saying,

"We all gave a bit of money for this for you and Ange, Sir. Good luck for the wedding on Saturday."

Wonderingly he opened it. Inside was a tooled silver pen tray with a glass, silver-topped inkwell fixed at one end. A beautiful scroll of flowers was etched into the glass. He knew Angie would love it as much as he did. Isla explained that her Mum loved Bargain Hunt on the tele and had helped her find it at the local antique shop.

In his turn he pulled out a big card with a fancy invitation on it for the whole group to come to the wedding at the church on Saturday and they cheered again as he passed it to Big Dave to look after.

oOo

When people haven't much in the way of a family, they say that the wedding will just be a quiet affair. Zak and Angie smiled at each other across the riotous gathering round the buffet in the church hall on Saturday lunchtime. Yes, the service had been thoughtful and moving, but now the hall was crammed with staff, friends, and the very boisterous story club. One of them seemed to have realised that there was a way they could still see Sir and Ange and perhaps hear more stories, so they were bending the ear of the rather bemused youth club leader. She couldn't believe they were about to get fifty new members all in one go!

The newly-weds had spoken to everyone but now attention was definitely on the food. With a meaningful look at his beautiful new wife Zak went into the men's loo while Angie went into the ladies' cloakroom. The travel bag with a lovely lavender trouser suit was still there so she slipped out of the long, slinky white wedding gown and left it on a chair. One of her friends in the know was to look after it for her. Picking up the bag she came out of the cloakroom to find Zak waiting and they went out of the back door into the car park. They by-passed Zak's old car, noticing the tin cans tied to it and all the sprayed foam and unlocked Angie's modest old Ford Fusion that no one had noticed. It had been parked on the road the night before ready for a quick, silent get-away.

It was not a long journey to Hunstanton where they had chosen to spend their four precious days of honeymoon before Zak had to prepare for his new job. Even so, by the time they reached the hotel the sun was a deep red and setting into the sea (the only place on the East coast where that could be seen) Their luggage was carried in and after a long, lingering kiss Zak took her hand and they stepped into their new life together.

NOTES

I hope you enjoyed this short book of stories within a story as much as I enjoyed writing it. If you have not already read "The Christmas of the Storyman", why not check it out. That and the "Columbae Peoples", set of three fantasy books can be found as paperbacks and Kindle e-books on Amazon.co.uk. You can look up my author page there too.

If cancer is an issue for you, see your GP as soon as possible. Don't trust Dr Google but you can find helpful information on the NHS website. That is where I found my information.

The full stories of the lives of the superheroes can be found in the Bible. If you put the names into an online search engine, it will tell you where to find their stories in the Old Testament of the Bible. You can also download free copies of the Bible online. The Good News Bible is an easy one to read.

There may be a third storyteller book out in late 2023.

Printed in Great Britain
by Amazon